Mark believes he's meeting Jimmy for the first time in the diner where he works, but he's wrong. Mark has no recollection of their original encounter because the wholesome Jimmy of today couldn't be more different than he was two years ago. Back then, Jimmy sported multiple piercings and facial hair. He was painfully skinny—and a meth addict. The drug transformed him into a lying, conniving thief.

Mark doesn't associate the memory of a hookup gone wrong with this fresh-faced twenty-something... but Jimmy knows. Can Mark see Jimmy for the man he is now and not the addict he was? The answers depend on whether true love holds enough light to shine through the darkness of past mistakes.

THE PERILS OF INTIMACY

Rick R. Reed

A NineStar Press Publication

Published by NineStar Press
P.O. Box 91792,
Albuquerque, New Mexico, 87199 USA.
www.ninestarpress.com

The Perils of Intimacy

Printed in the USA
First Edition
February, 2020

Print ISBN: 978-1-951880-32-3

Also available in eBook, ISBN: 978-1-951880-28-6

Warning: This book contains sexual content, which may only be suitable for mature readers, and graphic depiction of intravenous drug use.

For those struggling with the nightmare of addiction. May you find healing. May you find courage. May you find *love*...

You see, no one ever told me that as snakes shed skin, as trees snap bark, the human heart peels, crying when forced open, singing when loved open.

—*Mark Nepo, The Book of Awakening*

He brought me out into an open place; he rescued me because he delighted in me.

—*Psalms 18:19*

Monday

Chapter One

JIMMY

In romance novels, they call it *meet-cute*. If you're not familiar with the term or even with romance novels for that matter, let me explain. *Meet-cute* is how our two protagonists, our star-crossed lovers, if you will, first encounter the other. It might involve an embarrassing moment, or some great coincidence, or something like a setup, or a blind date that goes horribly wrong and does not bode well for the future. See...it's like there's that day where everything changes, often in a funny way, and our two love interests begin their journey toward love.

You might look at how Marc Kelly and I met as a meet-cute experience. It went something like this:

Even though I'm a smart guy, at least I think so, I've never really had much in the way of education. High school diploma was about it. I always hated school and never did very well in it, which is why I currently wait tables at a little diner in the lower Queen Anne neighborhood of Seattle. I've been at Becky's Diner a few years now, since I managed to get my life back in order. And I have to admit I like it. Becky's is the kind of place alcoholics end up at 5:00 a.m. for an eye-opener and, if their stomachs can handle it, maybe a couple of greasy fried eggs and some bacon. It's the kind of joint that's been in Queen Anne since the Depression and still looks like it—scuffed black-and-white tile floors, dark walls, red leatherette booths, and stools at the counter, many of them patched with duct tape. On the other side of the joint is a bar that's even darker—the drinks are strong, and we get a lot of regulars. The pinball machine over there pretty much goes untouched. Same with the TV, which is always tuned to some twenty-four-hours news crap with the sound turned off. No one watches it. Everyone's too busy nursing their drinks. Anyway, I wait tables in the diner part.

And I find myself digressing away from my meet-cute. Maybe that's because it wasn't really a meet-cute, but it makes for a good story. And that's what romances are all about, right? Good stories? At least on paper...

Anyhoo, about two weeks ago, this one guy comes in about seven, seven thirty. That day there hasn't been much of a breakfast rush—we're busier on the weekends—and I'm chilling behind the counter, checking Facebook on my phone. Marc, as I'd later find out his name, walks in, observes the Seat Yourself sign, and does just that—in the last booth at the rear. Right away, I see the guy is old school, as he spreads out an edition—paper, no less!—of the *Seattle Times*. He looks around expectantly.

I wipe my hands on my apron and approach, my order pad in hand.

I give him my trademark grin, the one I hope will coax big tips out of even the stingiest customers. "Hey there... mornin'! What are you in the mood for?"

He looks me up and down, a little smile twitching. I pick up on the gaydar, the attraction, and pause a little mentally because two things strike me almost simultaneously.

One: This guy is a good bit older than my twenty-three, maybe even by as much as fifteen or twenty years, but he's a hottie. DILF! His salt-and-pepper hair is full, nicely cut, side part, with more salt than pepper. He sports—rocks—a little goatee that's all salt. It perfectly frames cupid's bow lips. How's that for romance talk? But it's his eyes that floor me—so dark the pupils just about get lost in them. They grip me. They hold me. They make me wanna quiver.

Two: There's something about this dude that rings a bell. Not so much in the lust department, although that's definitely there in spades, but in the area of "Have we met before?" Because, yeah, he looks familiar. I just couldn't place him—at least not then.

We hold the look for a couple of seconds longer than the average waiter and customer would, and I can put my finger on this dance—it's called flirting. Gives me the warm and fuzzies inside, except for that nagging feeling that I know him from somewhere.

And when you have a past like mine, you want to be careful with shit like that. Because I've not always been the best person, to say the least. Anyway, that's something I've learned not to dwell on.

Can't undo the past!

All that stuff took, like, thirty seconds to go down. The guy speaks, "I'll have coffee and a cinnamon roll."

I pull a pencil from behind my ear. Not sure I'll need it, but just in case. "We're all out of cinnamon rolls," I say.

He grins, flips a page in the *Times*. Doesn't look up at me as he says, "Okay, then. I'll have tea." He flips another page. "And a cinnamon roll."

I chuckle. "We're all out of cinnamon rolls."

He nods and looks like he's taking what I just put down to heart. "Okay, uh, how about a glass of milk and...a cinnamon roll."

I shake my head. "Dude, I just told you—we're all out of cinnamon rolls. Sold out during the breakfast rush. But I'll tell you a little trade secret." I lean close to his ear and notice a very nice aroma coming off him—something tangy, piney, and manly. "The cinnamon rolls come from the QFC off Mercer. You can buy a four-pack for what you pay for one here."

"Okay," he says, looking into my eyes with those killer dark eyes. Those lashes! Man! "Just bring me a cinnamon roll."

I shake my head and then tuck the pencil back behind my ear. I start to head away, saying over my shoulder as I go, "You let me know when you're ready."

I can't decide if the guy is a cornball, a total asshole, or incredibly charming. He's probably a little of all three. And I feel a little flutter in my heart that tells me our little meet-cute encounter, which I've come to learn he lifted from some old public television kid's show, means he has his hooks in me.

Smitten.

And yet there's that nagging feeling I've met him somewhere before...and a darkness hides behind the notion that contradicts the fluttery feeling I get when I look at this hunk. In fact, that nagging recognition makes me a little sick.

It'll come to me. Or it won't. And something inside, a self-protective part maybe, hopes for the latter. They say ignorance is bliss, right?

He calls after me, "You do poached eggs? Runny?"

I turn. "We do anything. Two?"

He holds up two fingers and nods. "With coffee, no toast, no potatoes, fruit on the side if you got it."

I jot down the order. "No cinnamon roll?"

He just laughs and begins reading the paper.

When is a meet-cute not a meet-cute?

When you've met before.

And my gut drops a couple of inches as I remember where I met *him* before.

I don't want to go there. That was a different time. A different me. And there was nothing cute about it.

But I remember this guy because I felt something for him then. And I feel something for him now.

And it could never work.

Could it?

I watch from the corner of my eye as Cinnamon Roll, as I've dubbed him, downs his low-carb breakfast. How someone can eat poached eggs without any toast is beyond me, but it takes all kinds.

"You got a thing for him or what?" Matilda Blake, the other server on duty, whispers to me. She pauses just behind me with three plates balanced on two arms. I smell pancakes, bacon, and the sage aroma of sausage.

I turn a little to grin. "What?"

"Ah, don't play innocent with me, Mister. I could see the lust in your eyes from fifty paces."

I shrug. "Guilty. Maybe. A little."

She laughs, and it's a sound like a bell tinkling. Matilda doesn't even reach five feet and probably doesn't top ninety pounds, but she's a workhorse like you wouldn't believe. She has short, spiked blonde hair and numerous tattoos. On the weekends she plays in an all-girl metal band called Two Spirit. And in my head, I call her Tinker Bell, because that's who she looks like to me.

She takes off to serve her customers, but not without prompting me to "Go over and talk to him."

I busy myself filling ketchup bottles and the salt and pepper shakers I've removed from empty tables, but I keep an eye on Cinnamon Roll. His food is gone and the newspaper's been abandoned and he's staring off into space. I shudder because I wonder if he's recognized me and is thinking about our last encounter, a little over two years ago, at his place on Dexter Avenue.

But no, that couldn't be possible, could it? I'm a different person now, inside and out. Back then I was twenty, twenty-five pounds lighter than my current one hundred and sixty-five. I had a septum piercing like Ferdinand the Bull. My hair, which is now cut high and tight and is reddish brown, was long back then, bleached blond, dirty, and tangled up in dreadlocks that reached down almost to my waist. My skin had, I'm sure, a pasty and unhealthy pallor.

That person doesn't even exist anymore, and even though it's only been two years, I look completely different today. He's probably just thinking about his day or something.

Right?

I walk over to his table, a little nervous that he'd come to and look at me with an accusing glare. There'd be a scene. And maybe I'd end up getting fired or something. Thinking back to what I did to him, I deserve it.

But when I approach his table, all he does is smile. And that smile melts my heart. It did back then too. Just not enough to keep me from my desperate and dark ways.

"You need anything else?"

He looks down at his paper and back up at me. A blush rises to his cheeks, and I gotta say it—there's nothing more adorable than this face staring up at me right now. He looks like he wants to say something, but all that comes out is "The check? I gotta get to work. If I don't get out of here and on the bus, I'm going to be late."

"Oh?" I cock my head. "What do you do?"

"You don't want to know. Government contracts. Health care. Downtown. Websites, e-mail, so-called social media from a health-care perspective. Writing boring newsletters." He laughs. "Not the astronaut I thought I'd be back in kindergarten."

"Yeah. Well, I always dreamed I'd work in a diner. And look at me. Dreams do come true!" I tap my chest. "Living proof!" We stare at one another for a moment. My heart pounds for a variety of reasons, both sublime and shameful. "I'll get your check."

I turn and go to total up his modest bill. My hands are shaking just a tiny bit. There's this dark shadow of shame hanging over me that I try my best to banish. I remind myself that shadows are made by light and that I should direct my thoughts toward the light, not the darkness.

I look over at him once more. He's staring off into space again, and I take note of his clothes—the blue-and-white checked button-down shirt, the navy cardigan, the jeans with the rip in the knee of the left leg, the awesome wing tips, maroon and navy. He looks hipster professional. In the two years since I've seen him, he's hardly changed a bit. A little grayer maybe, but essentially the same guy. I get a quick vision of a big black leather headboard, framed in dark wood. A box on the dresser containing valuables...

His name comes to me in full. Marc Kelly. Simple. Solid. Like him. A good guy who never deserved what I gave him.

I should leave him alone. I know I should. No good can come from this.

A little voice inside reminds me I'm a changed person, one who loves himself, and I shouldn't beat myself up anymore. I should forgive myself and believe I'm deserving, especially now, of a man like this.

Still, it's with a lot of qualms that I write, near the bottom of his eighteen dollars and sixty-five cents total, Jimmy Kilpatrick (206) 555-9407. I pause for a moment, thinking I should tear this ticket up and write a new one.

No. I put one foot in front of the other, walk over to him, and set it in front of him. "You can pay up front. Thanks for stopping by."

I hurry away before he even has a chance to look down at the check or up at me. I head right through the kitchen and out the back door, where I stand outside by the dumpster in gray and drizzly February air and light up a smoke with shaking hands.

I think I have to release my wishes, to let them float away on the gray plume I exhale. I need to have faith—I remind myself—that everything will unfold just the way it should.

*

Much later in the day, after my shift, I head over a few blocks to a Methodist church and enter through a side door. It's a place I've become very familiar with over the past couple of years. Down a short flight of stairs, I'm in a big room with linoleum floors that are scuffed and never clean. Overhead fluorescents buzz and give the people gathered in the room a sickly yellow hue. There's a big picture of Jesus on the wall opposite. He's pulled his robe open to expose his heart, and I wonder, as I always do, if that hurts. Near the painting is a bulletin board filled with announcements about things like rummage sales, bingo, and people looking to unload unwanted cars, furniture, and roommates. There's a minikitchen along one wall, but we never use it.

I join a group of men and women, ten or so in all, seated in a circle on folding chairs. There's bad coffee and a box of doughnuts someone brought from Fred Meyer, standing open near the kitchen.

"Who wants to start?" Patrick, our de facto leader, looks around and asks. Patrick has always reminded me of the older African American Dr. Webber on *Grey's Anatomy*.

I speak up, because I'm anxious and need to *do* something, else I'll jump right out of my skin.

"Hi, everyone. I'm Jimmy, and I'm an addict."

Chapter Two

MARC

When I get to work, my check from Becky's Diner is burning a hole in my pocket. Who was this guy? And why did he assume I'd want his phone number? Was I ogling him that much? Is my gayness that obvious? And really, why does that even matter?

These and other paranoid, low-self-esteem thoughts plague me as I head up to the seventeenth floor and wander through a maze of cubicles to my own little corner of the professional world, near a back corner. I'm one of the lucky ones here at Panorama Health—I have a cube with a window. So I truly have a panorama—I can look over my shoulder and see Elliott Bay and, in the distance, West Seattle and the high-rises lining up along Alki Beach. I often sit here for longer periods than I should, watching the slow passage of a ferry across the impossibly blue water of the Sound.

But now I'm not distracted by the view. I sit down and take out the check, running my finger over the guy's name and number as though I'm reading braille. What difference does it make if he could tell I was gay? So what? He must be, too, if he gave me his number. And he must be interested! That last thought brings a smile to my face.

A head pops up over the cubicle. "What are you grinning about? For Christ's sake, it's Monday morning.

We're all supposed to be in the doldrums—or hungover from a weekend binge." It's Don Kurtz, administrative assistant to the communications department and my best friend here at work. He has the latter status not because he sits next to me—although that did help us get acquainted initially, back when I started here in the late 1990s—but because he has the most honest, and foulest, mouth I've ever run across. He's gay, too—a confirmed bachelor and former drag queen, back in his salad days in San Francisco—and older than me by about twenty years, but that doesn't stop Don from wanting to mother me. I pretend to resent that urge, but deep down I adore it. Maybe it's because my own mom is so far away, in Illinois—a Chicago suburb to be exact. And maybe Don wants to mother me because he's never had any kids of his own. Unless you count cats...

"Oh, this." I hold up my check from Becky's Diner.

Don comes over to my cube and snatches the greenish rectangle of paper out of my hand. He plops down in my guest chair and peers at it over the top of his glasses. He looks up at me, mystified. "What? You get a good deal on your breakfast?"

"Below that." I click my mouse to bring my keyboard to life and then key in a few strokes to establish that I am here and a part of the "family" at Panorama Health, Inc. I turn back to Don.

He's grinning. "Jimmy? Who's Jimmy?"

I laugh and feel a tiny bit of heat rise to my cheeks. I had thought I was too old for blushing. Apparently not. "A kid! He waited on me. He's young enough to be my son."

Don chuckles. "Well, apparently he has no issue with the age difference, so why should you?"

"I don't know. All of our cultural references are different. And apart from that—we move in different worlds. He's a waiter."

Don gives a mock shiver. "Heavens to Murgatroyd! God forbid we should consort with the hoi polloi!" He leans over to poke me in the chest. "Don't be a fuckin' snob. Just because he's salt of the earth doesn't mean he's dumb."

"You're right. You're right. I guess it's more the age thing that bothers me. I mean, I'm going to turn forty in a few months."

"And he's what? Twelve?"

I shake my head and roll my eyes. "No. But I'd put him in his early twenties."

"Go you! I am failing to see the issue here."

"He probably wants to call me Daddy."

"So? Rock your daddy status. Use it! Embrace it."

"Oh, Don, you're incorrigible."

He pats the top of his balding head as though he's fluffing a bouffant and does his best Mae West. "So I've been told." The impression vanishes quickly. "Did you feel something?"

I lean back. "What do you mean?"

"A spark. Get your mind out of the gutter! Did you feel a spark? When he looked at you and you looked at him, were violins playing?"

I scratch my goatee. "I think it was Demi Lovato."

"Whoever that is."

"Over the diner's speaker system."

He gently kicks my shin. "You're avoiding my question."

"Yeah," I say, staring at my monitor and feeling sheepish. "I guess. I mean, he was cute, *so* cute. With a tight little bod, auburn hair, and these beautiful blue eyes under heavy brows." I shake my head at the memory of him. "He just radiated something. I don't know."

"I think you *do* know. He was a hottie, and you liked what you saw. Nothing wrong with that."

"Yeah, there was that. But there was something more. Like, I don't know... I wanted to make him laugh. I wanted to see him smile. I wanted to..." my voice trails off as I try to take hold of exactly what I'd wanted when I saw Jimmy.

"Fuck him?" Don wonders, twisting the ruby ring he always wears on his pinkie around and around.

"You're crude."

"I calls 'em as I see 'em. Honey, I've been gay since before you were born." He pauses for a minute, calculating. "Well, maybe I'm not that old. But my point here is I *know* gay men. I know what we're like. We love sex! And there ain't nothin' wrong with that."

He has a point. I don't think of Don, pushing retirement age with a potbelly, as being a sexual being. But then I think that's not fair. And even if he's pretty celibate now, which I don't know for sure—nor do I want to—I know he had some pretty wild times back in the seventies when he lived in the Castro. But now? I think poor Don leads a pretty solitary existence. I know he has a woman friend, Esther, that he occasionally goes out to see a movie with, usually some tearjerker. But I also know much of his nonwork time is spent by himself. I tell myself I should leave it alone and just be grateful that he likes *me* so much. Because he's a hoot, and he brightens my otherwise dull and ordinary life.

"Yes, Don, there's that. In spite of the fact that he could be my son, if I started young. I just wonder what he sees in me, going to seed."

"Oh, cut it out! Do you know what I'd give to be forty again? Forty is *young*! And you are hardly going to seed. You're the best-looking guy in this hellhole." He looks around the office and then leans forward to whisper, "I'd fuck you myself if you ever showed a lick of interest in this old queen." He snorts. "I'd make your head spin like Linda Blair in *The Exorcist!*"

I clear my throat and feel a little embarrassed. "I think we established that. The first time we had too many margaritas at La Cocina."

He laughs with the memory of the very first time we went out to dinner together. He gets up. "I have work to do. Our fearless leader never stops e-mailing me with stuff to do. He keeps it up even over the weekend." He starts out of my cube and then comes back to whisper in my ear, "He needs to get that stick out of his ass and get a life."

We both laugh. He starts toward his own cube again. "So you gonna…"

"Call him?"

He nods.

"I don't know. Should I?"

"Honey, that's up to you. But I don't see any knights in shining armor exactly beating down your door. And you ain't getting any younger!" He snorts.

"Oh, I love you, Don. You build me up just to knock me down. At least you keep me on my toes."

"Oh, give him a buzz, for Christ's sake. What have you got to lose? Maybe this guy will keep you *off* your toes and get you on your back." He snickers as he walks away.

See why I like him? Well, maybe you don't. But there's just something, I don't know, bracing about Don that I find refreshing. It hits me suddenly—oddly—that this sixtysomething man, recovering alcoholic, potty mouth, sometimes drag queen, and cat lover is truly, deeply, madly—my best friend.

I look at the check again, then set it aside and get to work. I have a web page to update—all about avoiding bedsores in the nursing home setting.

Yay me.

*

It isn't until after lunch—and much goading from Don over bowls of pho—that I decide to man up and get in touch with Jimmy. I worry to Don that calling him this afternoon is too soon, that I would look too eager, desperate.

"Yeah, yeah. A lot of comfort that will be if you get hit by a bus later today. Honey, didn't I ever tell you? There's no tomorrow. Only a string of todays."

Dear Don. Always putting things in perspective.

I wrestle with my shyness for most of the afternoon, but at last, in that time between about three thirty and quitting—when my productivity plummets—I decide to take the plunge. Leap and the net will appear, as someone once said.

I grab my phone and head outside so I can have a little privacy. I know for a fact that Don will eavesdrop over the partition.

Not surprisingly, because it's February in Seattle, it's drizzling. The sky looks heavy, shades of charcoal and pearl gray. Traffic makes a hissing noise as it flows by on Seventh Avenue.

I huddle under the awning at the front of the building and kind of feel sorry for the smokers nearby, trying to indulge their habit and stay dry at the same time. They're not allowed to smoke within twenty-five—or is it fifty?—

feet of the entrance to the building, so they can't gather under the awning. All I can think is the need must be pretty powerful to want to stand in the rain and bone-chilling wind for a few puffs.

I look down at my phone and take in a deep breath and let it out slowly. I press the Home button to wake it up. I bring up the keypad and punch in Jimmy's number.

And pause.

Did I mention I was shy?

Probably yes. It's kind of an overriding theme for me. It's why I use those hookup sites to meet guys. I never have to *talk* to them. We can just message each other, maybe text. Even when we get together, often we don't have to say much of anything. It's no wonder I'm single at almost forty. The art of conversation and being engaging *still* eludes me. Online meeting—well, okay, hooking up—was the best and worst thing to ever happen to a shy gay man.

But that's another story. A whole essay. Maybe a book.

I realize I'm thinking to distract myself from the task at hand. Why is it so hard to actually *talk* to someone? I wish Jimmy had written an e-mail address on the check instead of a phone number.

I could text him.

No, don't take the chicken's way out.

And speaking of chicken, do I need to remind myself how young Jimmy is? A boy, really. Why, I wouldn't be surprised if he wasn't even of legal age for a drink.

Stop it.

I press the button to send the call out to Jimmy, out to the universe, out to putting thought into action.

I close my eyes, exhale with relief, and an unprovoked smile comes to my face when I get his voice mail. Voice mail I can deal with. There's no judgment there, no need to be clever or witty or charming. Just to-the-point. And that I can do.

"Hey, Jimmy. This is Marc Kelly, although I don't remember if I told you my name." I pause. Whatever. My palms are getting sweaty. Yes, even though this is voice mail. "Anyway... I'm the guy you waited on at Becky's this morning. You gave me your number?" I pause again, hoping I was not one of several guys he gave his number to. "So, uh..." What to say next? I hadn't planned it out. Why didn't I write down what I wanted to say?

Beeeeeep.

And the voice mail timed out. Now I have to call back. If I do, I sound like an idiot. If I don't, I'm a moron.

Just do it. I redial him and, without thinking, spit it out: "It's Marc again. Got cut off." I laugh in a silly manner, reminiscent of a teenage girl. "You want to, uh, meet up for a drink or maybe coffee sometime?" I say in a rush and then add, "Call me."

And then I hang up, quickly, like if I don't, the phone will explode or something.

On my way back up to my office in the elevator, I have a smack-my-head moment. I say aloud, "I never gave him my number." The woman in front of me turns to look at me, eyebrows together in confusion.

"Who?" she asks.

"Jimmy," I answer. I step off the elevator, feeling her eyes on me until the doors close.

And because I am now in the habit of talking to myself aloud in public, I reassure myself with "My number will show up on his Caller ID."

Back at my cube, I mumble, "Thank God for modern technology."

Don pops his head up over the cubicle wall. "What?"

Chapter Three

JIMMY

I don't notice I have voice mail until long after I get home.

Home is a closet-sized bedroom in the downtown-adjacent neighborhood known as Belltown. It can be—and is—a pricey area, but not for me. I live in a building on Western Avenue, not far from the Puget Sound waterfront, but the building is old and decrepit, and most of the tenants are Section Eights. Lightbulbs are out in the hallways, which are stinky with old cooking smells. The floors in the hallways are carpeted with some kind of worn fabric I've never been able to make out the color of because it's so dirty. The paint, in both the apartments and common areas, is a dingy yellowish-white that probably hasn't been updated for at least a decade.

It's depressing.

Still, it's home. I can walk outside my building and see the Space Needle to the north, the Sound to the west, the Ferris wheel, all the touristy sites. I can walk uphill and be in the heart of downtown in a few minutes.

A location like this—prime real estate, really—normally would command sky-high rents, but as I said, it's a kind of charity-ward building—and I don't say that unkindly—and I am the lowest of low an under-the-table renter in the apartment of a guy I met through my Narcotics Anonymous twelve-step group.

I've got my own little room and a shelf in the fridge and one in the kitchen cupboard. Bathroom privileges. That's it. And when I say "little room," I mean it. It's eight-by-ten, barely enough space for my single bed, a dresser, and a tiny computer desk my laptop sits on.

But for a mere $600 a month, it's all mine. Do you know what rents are like in Seattle? This is the deal of the century, folks.

I shrug and plop down on my bed, which squeaks loudly and once again feels in danger of collapse. I've tried to brighten up my cell—excuse me, room—with a few nice touches. My quilt, which I found at Goodwill, is bright red and yellow—some abstract pattern I find cheerful. I have a few posters tacked to the wall—mostly of vintage seventies and eighties album cover art that maybe my mom and dad once enjoyed. There's Soft Cell and the Stones' *Some Girls*, and a band called ABC, and an album called *The Lexicon of Love*. Someday I'll get around to looking up what a lexicon is. For now, I just like these pictures.

It's late, past midnight. After my meeting, I wandered around Queen Anne before walking home. I do that a lot. Wander. And think. Once upon a time, the wandering was to prevent me from using.

Using what? you might ask. And I would have gladly told you, once upon a time, because if I thought there was a chance you might be using, too, I'd be all over you, literally and figuratively, in the hopes that you had, as they say in the online ads, "favors to share."

I was once enraptured with, enfolded in the arms of, what we in the gay community call Tina, or Miss Tina if we're feeling really queeny. For those of you not in the know, Tina is shorthand for a particularly destructive and paradoxically exhilarating drug called crystal methamphetamine. It has taken the gay community by storm, and I once thought there wasn't a gay man alive who hadn't been caressed by Tina's toxic fingers. And when I say toxic, I mean it. That shit often contains a scary cocktail of things like battery acid, paint thinner, and other stuff you wouldn't imagine could get you high, only kill you.

Anyway, despite her nasty origins, I once conducted a long and irresistible love affair with Miss Tina, which I might tell you all about sometime. Or maybe I'll just share my first step from when I started going to Narcotics Anonymous and saving my life. I have it around here somewhere, right in this room. I pull it out and read it from time to time to remind myself how far I've come and why I never, ever want to go back there.

I did bad things.

The apartment is still. My roommate, a guy named Kevin, is asleep. He was once a vice president at a huge tech company—you've heard of it—until Tina got her claws in him, and he lost everything: husband, condo in South Lake Union, BMW, the works. He got HIV, bankruptcy, and a permanent tremor in his hands in exchange for all that. It allows him to get disability, so he calls it a fair trade.

Kidding.

But Kevin's quiet, and our paths, despite the small size of our place, seldom cross. He works now at a homeless shelter, where he once ended up living, helping out with cooking and cleaning three days a week. He can't work more than that or his disability amount will go down.

Ah. My world. Welcome to it.

I mention all of this only because when I at last lie back on my bed and pull my phone out of my pocket, I see I have voice mail.

A part of me is hoping it will be Marc, from the diner this morning.

Another part of me is terrified it will be him.

And that he will have remembered me. Despite how different I look. Despite the passage of two years in which everything changed for me—drastically and so much for the better.

Still, there's that past. No undoing that.

My finger hovers over the touch screen, not knowing if I want to bring the message to life or not. There's a sick feeling in my gut that I can't tell is anticipation or dread.

Of course, I can't stand it. I tap the screen to bring up the message. At this point I don't even know if it's him. It's just a number, local. It could be anyone. Someone from my twelve-step group.

The message plays. Ends abruptly. Then the next one rapidly follows. I smile. Running out of time on someone's voice mail is a maneuver I'd make.

Relief courses through me. He wants to see me.

And then the dread comes back. A stern little voice deep inside tells me, *He's gonna remember you eventually. And then he's not gonna like you so much. Just go ahead and hit Delete. Leave this poor guy alone. You hurt him enough, once upon a time. He won't forget that, even if you* have *changed.*

My fingers *do* hover over the red word Delete, but I can't bring myself to do it.

I want to see him. I'm thrilled that he thought to call me and couldn't even wait the space of one day to get in touch. I check the time on my phone. It's just past 1:00 a.m. It's too late to call back even though I want to.

I lay the phone down next to my head, imagining it's Marc. He once lay next to me.

"Hold me," I'd said. The image turns my stomach, and I clear it quickly with a rough shake of the head.

Do you believe in second chances?

Yeah, it's too late to call Marc back. But it's not too late to call my sponsor. Her number is at the top of my favorites list. You might think—or maybe you don't—it's odd for me to have a woman as my NA sponsor. And she's not even a friend of Dorothy! Just this suburban, rather straightlaced middle-aged woman from Bellevue, on the east side of town. A Republican. A fan of the books of Nicholas Sparks. A regular at the nail salon. A wife of a prominent attorney. A volunteer at a food bank in my neck of the woods.

And a drug addict. Miriam's dirty little secret—OxyContin—held her prisoner for years. She might have remained in that prison, refining her secrets and lies until her heart simply stopped, quieted finally by the drug. But fate intervened when she drove onto a crowded street corner in downtown Seattle. No one was killed. There were minor injuries.

But it woke her up in many ways; that was for sure.

When I started going to NA, Miriam was the first person to speak to me. I was quick to judge and tried to get away from her, in her sweater set, pearls, and pressed slacks, her beige pumps and pulled-back reddish hair.

What is her game? I'd wondered. *What does she want with the likes of me?* A super-skinny druggie with a septum piercing, bleached-blond dreads reaching scraggily halfway down my back, and a hollow, vacant stare.

But she was in a different place and knew what a smile, a word of welcome, and a hand on a shoulder could mean. If anyone should have judged someone by outward appearance, it should have been her judging me. After all, I looked like the homeless derelict I was. She looked like one of the 1 percent.

Thank God for Miriam.

She picked up on the third ring. "What's up, handsome?"

I pictured her getting gingerly out of bed, next to her sleeping husband, to take my call. I saw her move from the bedroom to stand somewhere else, maybe a tastefully appointed room with a desk and bookcases, looking out at the moonlight reflecting off Lake Washington.

I didn't know what to say, how to tell her. I cast around inside my own head for how to begin.

She came to the conclusion most sponsors would come to when confronted with a middle-of-the-night phone call, especially when the caller was having obvious trouble mustering up the courage to speak. "Hey," she said softly, her voice warm. "Are you using?"

One of our ground rules, when we'd first formed this sponsorship relationship, was a promise on both sides that we'd tell the other honestly whether we were using again. I was relieved I didn't have to answer her question in the affirmative.

"No. It's not that."

She blew out a little sigh—relief. "I'm glad to hear it."

"Would I mess up two years?"

"Oh, sweetie, I've seen people throw away twenty with a single moment of weakness. You know I wouldn't judge you if you had."

"I know. Thank you."

"So what's going on?"

"I met a guy." There's a lot of talk in NA meetings about romance and love, relationships. Addicts and love often do not mix, because when in the grips of something like Tina, no thing or person can hold a candle. And the secrets and lies? They're just toxic to a good relationship. Every twelve-step tradition I know of cautions against getting involved with anyone romantically until you have at least a year of sobriety under your belt.

Miriam says cautiously, "That's great, honey. What's his name?"

"Marc," I sigh and look around on my nightstand for my cigarettes and remember I smoked the last one before coming inside for the night. "But that's not the issue."

"What's the issue?"

I swear to God, I can *hear* her thinking, the wheels turning. If Miriam has one flaw, it's that she sometimes wants to help *too* much. She isn't good with simply listening, which is exactly what I need her to do right now.

She spits out her first assumption. "It's not too soon, you know. You've got two years under your belt!" she informs me. "Go for it!"

"I know. You're right. I shouldn't be afraid." I debate and debate and debate—should I tell her?

She rushes to conclusions again. "That's great! And he knows about you? And he accepts you?" She chuckles. "Why wouldn't he? You're a catch!"

I shake my head. I want to laugh, except the situation isn't funny. "You're not getting it, Miriam," I say, maybe a little too sharply. If she's anything, Miriam's big-hearted. I immediately regret my tone, that I let my impatience get the better of me. "Sorry. I didn't mean to snap at you."

I take a moment to compose myself, to think how to put things, and I hope Miriam won't rush in to fill the silence once again. I really need to talk to her tonight, and if I can't, I'll never get to sleep.

"I met him when I was using, like I said. It wasn't a pretty thing. We hooked up online, and I went to his place for sex."

"Okay…" In Miriam's world, I knew, such encounters probably didn't happen so much. Miriam herself had once told me she met her husband on a blind date set up by her sorority sisters.

"Gay guys do it all the time." I feel the need to explain. "Straight people too! Lots of people meet online now."

"I know. I know. Geez, I wasn't born yesterday." She laughs, and I feel a little embarrassed for underestimating her.

"Anyway, I was a different guy back then, as you know."

"Oh, I remember that guy." She goes quiet and then says, voice barely above a whisper, "He was lost."

"Yeah," I respond. "That's a nice way to put it. Anyway, the thing, the date, the hookup, whatever you wanna call it, didn't go well. In fact, it was disastrous. More for him than for me. I was so fucked up at the time, disaster was just an everyday fact of life, like the sun coming up in the morning." I pause, debating whether I want to tell her the whole story, what I actually did to Marc.

She wouldn't judge, but… I'm just not ready. Hell, I can barely chance glimpsing my own reflection in my memory mirror.

I go on. "The truth is I left his place with him probably kicking himself that he ever let me in his front door. And probably hating me with a passion."

"That doesn't sound good." She waits a second. "But I'm not putting this all together. Does he remember your night together or not? Because if he does—"

"Yeah. You got it. He doesn't remember me."

"Then you're in the clear. Sweetie, you are *not* the person I first met lo these many years ago. Not. At. All. You are a recovery story for the ages. I'm so proud of you."

I wish I could bask in her esteem. "I don't know if I'm in the clear. And thanks for the kind words. I'm just trying my best, just like you."

"Aww," she says.

I scratch at my back and go on. "He *could* remember. I think he doesn't because I look so different. But I'm still me, you know? Different hair, no nose ring, weight piled on—I certainly don't match up to what I used to put out there. And we just met the one time, and *that* was two years ago. But still..."

"You worry?"

"Yeah." I tell her how Marc came into the diner that morning and I waited on him. I tell her I felt something for him even back then, and even though I was fucked up, and it was far from magic but closer to criminal, I never forgot him.

"I know I should walk away. Forget him." I shake my head in my dark little bedroom, pretty sure I don't have *that* much strength.

"You're being too hard on yourself," Miriam says.

"I don't know if I am. I *hurt* the guy."

"Yeah, I hurt lots of people when I was using too. Now you tell me—does that mean I should suffer for the rest of my life for what I did?"

"But you don't know what I did to him..." I shudder just a tiny bit at the sound of myself, the whining.

"I wasn't asking a rhetorical question, JD."

"No one calls me that anymore. That was the old me."

"Okay. I wasn't asking a rhetorical question, *Jimmy*." She takes a breath and goes on. "I forgot to pick my kids up at school one time—left them for hours. I was high. I almost burned down our house once when I left a pot of tomato soup simmering on the stove and fell asleep on the couch. I forgot birthdays, holidays. Heck, I forgot who I was at times.

"And you know what? My big accident—my *hitting bottom moment*—wasn't my first accident." She laughs, but there's little mirth in it. "They knew me by name at our body shop. But getting back to my question—do you think I should suffer forever for what I did back then?"

"No, of course not. You've cleaned up. You've made amends. You help me. You help other people. You're good, Miriam. Real good. I want to be like you when I grow up."

She laughs. "So, let me get this straight—you'd forgive me for all the crap I pulled when I was high and running around like *Nurse Jackie*?"

"Yeah, yeah, of course."

I listen to her breathing. It's like she's waiting. And then she says, "Then why wouldn't you forgive *yourself*, Jimmy?"

The idea hits me—hard, causing tears to spring to my eyes. I have no answer. I could easily forgive other people for screwing up, for hurting others, for doing bad things, wrong things. But why couldn't I find that same forgiveness in my heart for myself? Why did I think so little of *me* that I couldn't even consider forgiving *me*?

I sigh. "I guess I should." I say the words, but I don't know if my heart is convinced. And I wonder again: do I hate myself? Or do I hate myself *that much*?

Wasn't hating myself exactly why I used in the first place? To escape? Because I didn't think enough of myself to treat myself better? I shudder.

"You've given me a lot to think about, Miriam. Thank you." I'm guessing sleep isn't in the cards tonight. Maybe I'll walk over to the convenience store down the street and pick up some smokes. I can wander around the waterfront and ponder.

"It's not really so much to think about, hon. One thing I've learned is we humans, with our monkey minds, tend to overcomplicate, when life really is so simple. Love yourself, Jimmy. With all your heart. That's the only way you'll ever find real happiness.

"We all make mistakes. But I always remember what *my* sponsor told me—mistakes are the soil we grow from. Every mistake, every bad thing we did, shouldn't be a regret because everything we do is simply one more step on our journey. Without the mistakes, we'd never grow."

"You're right." I know I'm still not entirely convinced. The old me, the addict me, probably doesn't want me to be. *And why is that?* I ask myself. Because that's just the kind of thinking that would lead next to me asking— *Where can I score?*

"Just believe, right down to your little toes, that you're a good person. You deserve love. You deserve forgiveness. Especially from yourself. Now step into the present, stay here, and just go to sleep. That's what I'm going to do."

And she simply hangs up. Miriam's like that. When she's said her piece, she's done.

My current addiction—nicotine—is calling. And my need to be out and about on the dark and still late-night streets beckons.

But before I go, I act impulsively. After all, the phone is still in my hand. Without giving myself a chance to second-guess, I quickly text:

Hey Marc. Hope I didn't wake u. Love to see you sometime. Call me in the morning. Jimmy.

I hit Send before my monkey mind steps in and tells me I'm being rash, or before the self-loathing part tells me I don't deserve to explore where things might go with this good and handsome man. That part has names for me. *Impulsive. Reckless.* I cling to what Miriam said and think that I'm just going after good.

Good that I deserve. I can choose good or I can choose bad. I choose good. I choose happy.

Yeah, now I just have to make myself believe that.

I get up from my bed and creep silently from the apartment, my phone tucked hopefully into my back pocket, longing for the twinkling tone notifying me I have a text message.

Tuesday

Chapter Four

MARC

The sun peels my eyelids open. I sit up in bed, surprised, shaking my head a little and finally smiling. A little song of unexpected joy dances a jig in my heart.

Waking to sun in February in Seattle is a rare and wondrous thing.

It's also an alarming thing when it's a workday. When the sun *does* deign to come out, it isn't until after seven thirty or so. Which means I have little to no time for getting ready for work and certainly none to stop for a leisurely breakfast at Becky's Diner. Before I went to bed last night, I'd thought about doing just that. It was a pleasant thing to look forward to as I toddled off to my room after binge-watching four episodes of *The Good Wife* on Amazon.

No worries. I just need to hustle through the morning routine, skip breakfast—at least until I can get to the office, grab Don, and head down to the Starbucks on the concourse level of our building—and manage to catch my bus across the street on Dexter Avenue.

I hurry through the routine, skipping shaving—hey, the stubbled look is hot, right?—and getting in and out of the shower in five minutes flat. A quick brush of the teeth and a floss and I'm ready to pick out my clothes for the day. Piled atop my bedroom chair are several pairs of previously worn jeans and shirts, almost all of them T-shirts. We're casual at Panorama but not that casual. I rifle through the top shelf of my closet until I find a comfortable old gray ragg wool sweater, pairing it with a white button-down shirt, black jeans, and black Chuck Taylors.

I hurry out the door of my apartment building, pausing for a moment when I hear the sound of an air horn blasting on Lake Union. A little to the north, almost magically, the Fremont bridge will raise itself so a boat with a high mast can get through. I like the sound. It reminds me I live near the water.

Ah! My green-and-gold #62 Metro transit bus is just now making its way southbound up the hill toward me. I'm grateful it didn't get held up by the bridge and grateful that timing seems to be on my side today.

I look both ways and dash across the street, dodging the flow of cyclists on their way downtown in the bicycle lane. I swear some of them look at pedestrians as competition—blood sport. I make it to the other side as a bicyclist comes straight at me, then swerves dramatically to miss me at the very last second. How dare I set foot in the bike lane, interrupting his course! I consider giving him the finger but let him off the hook because I see the bus is almost there.

No harm. No foul. We are all where we're supposed to be, at the right time.

Once on board, I pull my phone from my pocket and see there's a text. I open it and think I have one more reason—in addition to the sunshine and this morning's perfect timing—to grin.

Jimmy has gotten back to me! And the same day! That's a good sign, right? None of this waiting around for some weird "appropriate" time to pass before getting in touch. God forbid someone should appear too eager. God forbid someone should actually know they're liked in return.

His message is sweet and simple—to the point, just as I imagine him to be. Just as I hope he is. My sad story is that the men in my life have come with more baggage than a cargo hold on an Alaska Airlines plane. It would be refreshing to get with one who doesn't know the meaning of "it's complicated."

I'm glad he texted instead of called. For one, seeing the time stamp on the text, if he'd called, he'd have woken me up. For another, I'm a hopeless introvert. Texting was the best thing that ever happened to electronic communications, in my opinion. I never, ever like talking on the phone. Just contemplating it sometimes can set my heart to pounding and palms to sweating.

Texting gives us a measure of ease, some time to think about what we want to say and how to say it. And even though Jimmy said to "call" him, I figure his message to me means he won't look down on me for texting back. Besides, I'm not about to have a conversation with *a boy I like* on a crowded bus full of strangers. Sure, they're all hunched over their own smartphones and tablets, even the ones standing in the aisle, but I get nervous enough about talking on the phone without the added stress of thinking someone might be eavesdropping.

So I tap out a quick text back. Something—maybe the rare winter sun—has put me in a good, and bold, mood. Waking up late and being in a rush seems to be sending a message to me that life is short, and if I want something, I need to grab it. No hesitation. What's that old poem say? *Gather ye rosebuds while ye may?*

I also figure I have nothing to lose. I ignore the mom voice in the back of my head that's always there, buried deeper at some times than others, telling me that when you feel you have nothing to lose, that's the precise moment when you have *everything* to lose. It's like asking "What could possibly go wrong?" It's reckless. Heedless.

Shut up, superego. I want to see the guy again, and not when he's serving me breakfast.

Unless it's breakfast in bed... I accompany the thought with a Groucho Marx eyebrow wiggle.

Hey you... You didn't wake me because it's morning. Looks like you're a night owl.

I pause, wondering just how stupid I sound. I glance out the window at yet another high-rise building going up on Dexter. It seems like every other day they start building a new one, the downtown mushrooming north on my street.

What do all those buildings have in common? I ask myself. Hope. They're all built with many things, but I bet you every one of them was predicated on the simple fact of hope. So I know I need to banish my self-doubt, be confident that my own stupid self is the only one I have, and doggone it, it's good enough. And I need to hope:

That he still thinks I'm cute.

That he wants to see me again.

That my offer of a date real soon will be music to his ears.

You working tonight? If not, do you want to meet up for a drink? Dinner?

My finger hovers over the little blue Send letters. Hopeful as I am, cheerful and optimistic as I view myself right now, I still have little gnats of doubt and maybe even dread hovering about the perimeter of my confidence.

Am I being too quick?

Too pushy?

Do I sound desperate?

So what if I do? So the fuck what? I ask myself.

If I don't do this, what are the odds I'll be sitting across a table from Jimmy tonight? Zero. Those are my chances.

If I overthink how I'm coming across in a frigging text, how am I going to be able to even string together a coherent sentence when we are together, assuming he says yes?

Before I have a chance to decide for myself whether I'll revise and rewrite, the bus lurches to a sudden stop, sending all the passengers in the aisle grabbing on to the handgrips, and in some cases each other, for support. One woman screams.

I look up and see that a bulldozer has lurched into the road in front of the bus. A hunky construction worker, all hirsute and swarthy, is holding up a stop sign.

Bikes whiz around us.

And I look down to see that the universe has made a decision for me. The sudden halt of the bus caused my finger to touch the screen, sending my message off.

It was meant to be.

I look out the window, squinting at the sun, and realize I'm smiling.

*

When I get to work, Don's waiting for me in my cube. He's looking down at his watch and tapping the face. "You're late," he says, with a big grin to show he's only kidding.

But it's true. In spite of my best efforts, I'm ten minutes late. If our boss had seen me skulking through the network of cubes to my own home away from home, he would have given me one of his trademark frowns of disapproval that are just perfect because he's had so much time and so much practice in getting them just right.

"Yeah, yeah." I wave Don away with my hand and then sling my messenger bag onto my guest chair. I stoop over my computer to log in. I quickly scan my e-mails to make sure there's nothing urgent, like a midnight missive from the boss with something that *must* get done before 9:00 a.m. He's done it before. I don't think the man ever sleeps.

Or ever disconnects from work e-mails.

But there's nothing earth-shattering there. So now that I'm late for work, why not compound the tardiness by immediately leaving my desk to disappear downstairs for fifteen or so minutes?

I smile at Don. "Starbucks run?"

"Why do you think I'm standing in here waiting for you? Honey, you're not that irresistible." He rubs his potbelly. "Those blueberry muffins in the bakery case are not gonna eat themselves." He sighs and heads off toward the elevators just past our lobby. He knows I'll follow.

"He texted me. Last night," I say to Don as we stand off to the side from the ordering line at Starbucks, me waiting for my smoked butterscotch latte and he for his Americano and warmed blueberry muffin.

"Who? Chris Hemsworth? Because if that bitch called you before me, I am going to strangle him."

I laugh. "You're too much."

"Well, how should I know who this mystery man is who texted you! Jesus, for a while there, you were hooking up with every Tom and Hairy Dick in town on Adam4Adam." He wags his eyebrows at me. "Has that changed?"

"It changed months ago. You know that."

"Yeah, when you got, what was it, chlamydia?"

I look around before I push him lightly. "Shut *up*!" I glance around again, but everyone is consumed with getting their caffeine fixes. "Someone could hear you."

"Over that espresso machine? I highly doubt it. Besides, in my day, venereal diseases were a badge of honor."

"That's not true. And no one calls them venereal diseases anymore."

"Okay. Sexually transmitted disease. STD. How's that?"

"Still wrong. The cool kids are calling them STIs these days, short for sexually transmitted infections."

"Charming." Don moves up because his name has been called. I watch as his eyes light up when he claims his Americano and muffin. I know there will be exactly four packets of sugar added to his coffee.

"Anyway," I say in his ear as I step up beside him to nab my own order. "The waiter I told you about yesterday?"

"Ah. Yes. The little boy who's far too young for you."

"Right. That's the one. Why is it you always remember the wrong stuff?"

"It tickles me," he says, heading for the condiments counter to load up on sugar.

We finish doctoring our caffeinated beverages, he with sugar and me with half-and-half, and head back upstairs.

He throws my messenger bag on the floor and drops into my guest chair to have his breakfast and a chin-wag. I know he'll spew crumbs everywhere. I will wait until he's back in his own cube and at work—finally—to quietly clean them up. I know all of this because this is usually how we spend the first hour of work here every day, unless something trifling and annoying crops up like a staff meeting or, you know, actual work.

"So what did he say?" Don asks.

"He wants to get together."

"Do the horizontal bop?"

I shake my head. "It's not always about sex." I open the messenger app on my phone to bring up Jimmy's text.

"It's always about sex, honey. I would think you, Miss Chlamydia of 2017, would know that." He giggles.

I shudder. "Will you shut up about that? I'm sorry I ever told you." I show him the screen. "See? 'Love to see you.' Does that sound like a booty call to you?"

Don snickers. "Honey, it's been so long since I've had a booty call, I'm not sure I'd know what one sounded like."

"Well, that's your own fault. You need to get out more." I look him up and down and feel a little sad. Don is about forty pounds overweight, balding, with a kind of wizened, pinched face that makes him appear even older than he is. Picturing him lounging at the Cuff or the Eagle just sends the pathos meter in my heart skyward. I love the guy. I really do, but I also know how youth and beauty obsessed other gay men can be. In short, I know why he no longer goes out, even though he never says.

"Maybe next weekend, I'll do a bar crawl with you."

"Okay. That's the spirit." I know it'll never happen. Next weekend he'll do what he always does—order a Pagliacci pizza and watch some old Douglas Sirk movie on Netflix. Drink a bottle of red wine. Cry himself to sleep. If he gets any action, it'll be courtesy of Pornhub on his computer. I know all of this because he's told me. Secretive, Don is not.

"Anyway, I texted him back that maybe we could grab

a drink or a bite to eat." I put my coffee down on my desk and smile. "Tonight."

"Oh! Look at you. Mr. Proactive! Mama's so proud. And no questions about top or bottom or what he 'likes'?"

I grin. "Not yet. I like to ask those in person."

"When you're bent over in front of a guy?"

I'm tempted to say that when I'm bent over in front of a guy, such questions would be redundant. Instead I just sigh and turn to my computer to wake it up. Over my shoulder, I say, "Oh, look here. I have a meeting to get ready for. It's in fifteen minutes."

"You're a liar. And I get it." He gets up and wanders away. The easy thing about my friendship with Don is that he knows when he pushes over the line.

I pull out my phone and check to see if any new text messages have come in. I do that every fifteen—okay, every ten—minutes throughout the day until, at last, my diligence and persistence get rewarded.

I'd love to see you—dinner, drinks, coffee, whatevs. Just shoot me a time and a place, and I'll be there.

Really? I stare dreamily away from the phone, knowing there's a grin spreading across my face. I curtail it suddenly when I have a bad thought. You know that saying—if something sounds too good to be true, it probably is?

That's how I feel about this. I know I shouldn't. I should just look at what I have here and not what I lack. I should be happy instead of wary—because things are turning out just the way I'd like them to.

But a lifetime of disappointments—especially in the romance department—has kind of conditioned me toward being a pessimist. I mean, if you look at the parade of losers who have marched in and out of my bedroom—

druggies, thieves, poseurs, liars, cheats—you'd sympathize. I really think you would.

I shake my head and glance out the window. The day has remained sunny, and the light falls in slants down on the Sound, which looks slate blue and churning just a bit from the wind. I shouldn't do this to myself. Those self-help books that have accumulated on my Kindle all say the same thing: basically, perception shapes reality. Our minds and what we choose to focus on really do determine how our lives go.

So I can choose to look at Jimmy as just another loser in a long line of losers and conclude, before I even give him a chance, that things will go to hell in a handbasket, and I'll come away licking my wounds and wishing I'd never met him.

Yeah, I can choose that. And that choice will most likely be reflected on my face as soon as we sit across from each other, face-to-face. And that attitude will carry through, becoming a self-fulfilling prophecy.

See what I mean?

Or...

I can look at Jimmy's message—so positive, so eager, so cheerful and guileless—as a sign that things are turning around for me. That things are going right. That maybe I've been able to meet a guy who's not only younger than I have a right to, but who's also hot and actually a nice person. I could anticipate good times ahead rather than dread bad ones.

Where's the harm in that?

Where indeed?

I have nothing to lose, really, by accentuating the positive. In fact, maybe I can encourage the good to happen by believing in it.

I text him back, swatting away that buzzing, annoying

thought that pops up in the back of my brain like a gnat, and decide to simply be positive and proactive. And immediate.

How about tonight? Dinner? Café Mecca? 6:30?

I can't be much clearer, or more positive and specific than that. I hit Send.

Before I even set my phone down, it makes its little chime, letting me know I have a text. I look down to see:

Sure. I look forward to it. See you there, handsome.

I smile and laugh a bit to myself, staring at the screen. My laugh must've been louder than I thought because a nasal voice comes at me from the top of the partition that joins Don's and my cubes.

"You watching porn again?" he whispers. "Group scene? You can tell me."

I just shake my head. He hurries around the partition, and I hand him my phone, on which the messages are still up.

He sits in my guest chair and quickly scans. He hands me back the phone. "So lover boy has a date. And tonight? Already? Are you gonna have time to get home and douche?" He snickers.

I'd give him a hard time, but I have a sneaking suspicion he's a little jealous, so I'll let him slide.

"It's a first date, Don. No reason to douche. I'm not like that anymore. Remember?" I don't know if the statement is really true. But it's fun to tease Don that I am. It hadn't even occurred to me yet, which I suppose is a bit of progress, that the upcoming evening could end on a sexual note. I was just happy about my good fortune—everything was working out the way I wanted it to. Oh, and looking forward to seeing Jimmy's smiling face again.

I know in the past, my first thought would have been

Am I gonna get laid tonight? and it makes me worry that I'm becoming an old man...prematurely. I am, after all, only almost forty. In a few months—let's not rush anything. And as Don says, "Forty is young."

Or maybe the direction my train of thought is traveling in isn't a sign of age or waning sexual desire, but of maturity.

"I don't remember a thing, you whore." He smiles to soften the name-calling, and I grin back. The reason Don is my best friend is because, not despite, we can say the most horrible things to each other and know it's all in good fun and, most important, out of love. "But six thirty? Does that even give you time to get home and change?"

"Why do I need to change? I look fine." I'm wondering if my clothes are too wrinkled or if the day has created bags under my eyes, if I simply look tired...and twenty years older than my prospective date.

And for once, Don isn't mean or snarky or biting. He leans forward a little. "You do look fine." He eyes me up and down. "More than fine. Hot." He leans a little closer and whispers, "And I hate you for it."

Chapter Five

JIMMY

"You look fine. Better than fine. Sweet. Hot." My roommate, Kevin, gives me the once-over. "I like that T-shirt. Where'd you get it?"

I glance down at my Rat City Rollergirls black tee and note how it hugs my chest and grin. "That thrift store on the Hill. I forget the name. The one on Broadway."

"Oh yeah, they have good stuff. Great for Halloween." We're in the kitchen, and Kevin is making himself dinner—bologna and Velveeta cheese on white bread with pickles and yellow mustard. Just looking at it makes me want to hurl.

But I hold back my gag reflex. We will not entertain why my gag reflex is, for the most part, nonexistent. We will not go there. "So I look okay?"

Kevin sighs and nods. "Oh, quit fishing." He takes a bite of his sandwich and sets it on the counter. I have never seen the man actually sit to eat. He turns to rummage around in one of the cupboards and brings out what I assume is his vegetable side dish—a bag of Cool Ranch Doritos. He pulls a handful out and sets them on the plate next to his sandwich. He points to his supper. "Now that's a balanced meal. You got your starch, your protein, and your corn."

"If you say so." I grab a Dorito from his plate and pop it into my mouth. They *are* good.

He pours himself a glass of store-brand cola from a can in the fridge and tells me, "You're what? Twenty-five?" Kevin himself could be anywhere between thirty and forty. He's skinny, nondescript—everything on him is in various shades of beige—and almost invisible.

"Twenty-three," I correct him.

"Okay." He takes a sip of cola. "When you're twenty-three, you look good even if you don't look good. You get me? Youth is always on your side. Even when you put all the crap you put in your body."

"Which I don't anymore," I remind him, maybe a little too harshly.

He holds up a hand in supplication. "I know, I know. And I'm proud of my little recovery poster child. My point is, Jimmy, you couldn't look bad if you tried. You not only have youth on your side. You have good health. Vitality. And though it pains me to say it 'cause I know it'll go straight to your head, you're the kind everybody in the bar hopes they'll go home with. Which is why they wait until 3:00 a.m. to settle for the likes of me." He laughs, but there's a bitter edge to it.

"Don't talk about yourself that way."

He waves me away with a sandwich-bearing hand. "Ah! I gave up on illusions about my looks the same time I gave up meth." He grins. Even his teeth are beige. Thank God I didn't do enough crystal, or do it for long enough, to have it mess up my teeth. "As Popeye says, 'I yam what I yam.'" He cocks his head. "And I'm good with that. You know?"

"I do know." I nab another Dorito, and as I pull my hand away, Kevin slaps it. "You're going out for dinner!

You're probably getting laid tonight. Can't you let me have my junk food supper in peace?"

I chew up the Dorito and swallow. "Sorry. Never could resist those things."

He shoves the bag toward me, and my hand snakes inside, grabbing more. "I don't know about that last part, though."

"Getting laid?"

I nod. "Yup."

"What do you mean? You're young, hung, and full of come. Or at least that's the word on the street."

I snicker. "It's been a while. You should know that. Your bedroom is next to mine."

"Honey, that don't mean nothin'. Time was, when I was getting high, doing it in the bedroom was an oddity. I was more likely to be behind some bushes in a public park or at some adult bookstore or the baths. A bedroom? How quaint! How very Renee Zellweger in *Bridget Jones's Diary*!"

We both crack up. It's good I live with Kevin. Even though he's usually as quiet as *To Kill a Mockingbird*'s Boo Radley, Kevin is good for me because he understands the horror of addiction and we can laugh about it. There aren't many folks in the world I can find that in common with. It's really a blessing.

Certainly not my date tonight. Marc doesn't do drugs. Or at least he didn't the last time we were together—the time I'd rather not think about. I know, because I tried to tempt him.

My gut gives this little queasy lurch, and I taste bile splashing up at the back of my throat. And it's not because of Kevin's sandwich.

"What? You just turned white." Kevin puts his sandwich down.

I let out a shaky sigh and lean against the counter. Suddenly this date seems like a very bad idea. "I shouldn't go," I mumble.

"What? Why? I thought this guy was really cute and you liked him a lot."

"I know, but I barely know him." I look down at the worn red linoleum of our kitchen floor just as a cockroach scampers by. I think about stomping on it but decide to let the creepy critter live to see another day. I'm magnanimous like that.

Kevin knows a lot of my story. And he sure as hell understands how crystal meth can turn someone into a completely different person—selfish, narcissistic, reckless—so he doesn't hold my history of homelessness and sometimes crime against me. He knows the Jekyll-and-Hyde effect of the drug on people, knows it firsthand, so he wouldn't judge. But still, this coincidence of running into Marc, a former trick from back when I was using, an innocent bystander I did wrong, seems like too much to share with my roomie. If I don't even like looking the demons from my past in the eye, how can I expect Kevin to?

I don't want to talk about it. "Ah, never mind. Just having first-date jitters." *Even though it's not technically a first date*, I remind myself. I practice what Miriam told me to do when I feel stressed. *"It's simple, sweetie. What you need to do is* breathe. *In through the nose—deep breath—and out through the mouth. Do that a few times, and I promise you'll calm yourself."* So I do what she told me and—what do you know—it works. I feel calmer, a little more in control. "Things are gonna be okay," I say to Kevin, who's just about to head into his own room to do whatever he does on his personal laptop.

"Of course they are." He puts the loaf of bread back in the cupboard, along with the chips, and then puts the sandwich fixings into our fridge. "Have fun. And be careful. You sure this guy isn't a user, right?"

Other addicts know too well how even the smallest thing can act as a trigger. He's making sure about Marc because he cares.

"Positive," I say. *More sure than you know*, I think.

"Good. Even when you haven't been around any triggers for a while, all it takes is some little something—can be really tiny—to flip a switch in your brain. And then—*poof*—it's all gone."

"I know, I know."

"Gonna watch a little *Orange is the New Black*."

"You have fun. I'll tell you all about it later."

As he walks away, I shudder. Will I regale Kevin with a story of a wonderful and romantic evening with a warm and sexy man? Or will I be sorrowful, spilling out a confession because Prince Charming, whom I'm meeting in less than an hour at Café Mecca, recognized me from his past and, naturally, wanted nothing to do with me?

Ever.

I sigh, ready to roll the dice. I grab my denim jacket from a hook by the front door and head out.

Chapter Six

MARC

My mother, back in the Chicago suburb of Skokie, Illinois, always told me that being on time was the same thing as being late. "You want to be on time, you get there fifteen minutes early." She lived by those words and expected my dad and two sisters to live by them too. She drilled the idea of punctuality into us so thoroughly we were all anal about it.

I mention this so you understand why I'm sitting in a booth at one of my favorite dives, Café Mecca in the lower Queen Anne neighborhood, at six when my date isn't scheduled to arrive until six thirty.

I had an interesting walk over here, strolling from downtown along Fifth Avenue, underneath the monorail for a lot of the way. The weather, in addition to the sky turning from day to night in what seemed like a few minutes, also went from being temperate-for-winter to drizzly and bone-numbingly chilly, more because of the damp than due to the change in temperature. Even though Seattle seldom gets down to freezing in the winters, it's the damp that seems to penetrate into you, no matter how many layers you wear.

Whatever. I ordered a coffee when I got here, and for something to do, I'm looking at the crap plastered to the hanging light fixture over our table—mostly stickers from grungy bands—and the old menus affixed to the wall to my right, from when the Mecca first opened back in the late 1920s. It's amazing what a couple of bucks would once buy. Even in a dive like this, I know dinner for two will easily run forty bucks or more.

The waitress, a chubby redhead with a diamond nose ring, returns to the table. She puts a hand on a hip, sighs dramatically, and asks, "Stood up? *Again?*" She laughs. Her laugh, like her smile, like her very presence, radiates warmth.

I decide I like her. Maybe I should quit my corporate job and get a position waiting tables. I seem to have developed a taste for restaurant servers lately. I glance down at my watch. "It's only twenty after. He's not even supposed to be here until six thirty."

She tops off my coffee. "He? He? Seriously?" She sighs. "There go *my* dreams." She bats her lashes at me, and I smile. "I'm sure he'll be here soon. I doubt anyone would want to stand you up, mister."

"Oh, you'd be surprised."

"I would," she says. "I really would." She walks away.

I do start to get a little worried when six thirty arrives and no Jimmy. At 6:40, no Jimmy. At six forty-five, the door opens and I look up, hopeful, as I have every time the door opened for the last half hour, and see only a middle-aged gay male couple standing there, waiting. They're kind of sweet. I can immediately tell they're together—their rapport with each other is easy and familiar. I overhear a few words—*cheat day* and *french fries with gravy.*

I envy them.

As Big Red, as I've come to call her, though only mentally, leads them to a booth behind me, I spy Jimmy enter.

My heart beats a little faster for a couple of reasons. One—he's here! He did show up, even if he is late, really late by my mom's standards. And isn't there some saying about 80 percent of success coming from showing up? The bar is low in our world, especially in mine. But he's here! Second—I'm just happy to see him and to know he's not only shown up, but he came to see me.

I smile and sort of half stand as he approaches. He looks good, in a beat-up denim jacket, gray cargo pants, black boots, and a black Rat City Rollergirls T-shirt. If I had a favorite roller derby team, Seattle's Rat City girls would definitely be it, mainly because I don't know of any other roller derby teams. His eyes meet mine, and they're clear and a shade of blue that reminds me of the water in Elliott Bay.

"Hey, stranger," I say softly, extending my hand.

He grips it, and his grip is firm but not bone-crunching. My father taught me that you could tell a lot about a man from the way he shook your hand. Jimmy seems confident and warm, sure of himself.

But then, I suppose, so do I. I just know how to properly shake hands is all. On the inside I'm nervous, once again thinking how I'm way too old for this pup. What on earth does he see in me?

He slides in across, and I blurt it out before I have a chance to censor myself. "You smoke?" I mean, I don't really need to ask. The smell of cigarettes surrounds him like a cloud. Usually a guy being a smoker is a deal-breaker for me, but I don't know, maybe I could make an exception? People can change, after all.

He looks down at the table and smiles both sheepishly and charmingly. He looks up at me as he struggles. "Yeah. Do I stink?"

I shrug. "Maybe a little. It's okay."

"I'm glad you don't. At least one of us is clean."

"That's an odd thing to say. How do you know I don't?"

He sets his jacket to the side, and I can tell he's thinking about how to respond. After a moment he says, "I don't smell anything on you." He leans forward, nose twitching. "Except maybe a little, uh, what is that, anyway?"

"Tom Ford," I answer. "My mom gave it to me for Christmas. I hope you're not one of those guys who's anti cologne?" I pick up the paper napkin on the table. "I can wipe it off."

Jimmy wiggles his eyebrows. "Maybe we can shower together later...get the stink off both of us."

I laugh but realize his little flirtation embarrasses me. I know because I feel heat rise to my cheeks.

"Ah! Look at you!" He points. "You're blushing."

"Sorry." I stare down at the menu, face heating up even more. And then I feel his hand on mine. "I was just teasing. It's cute. I don't see blushing much anymore. I think it's charming. And kind of sexy." He gives my hand a little squeeze before pulling away. My face feels even hotter, if that's possible. And things are stirring farther south. I take a gulp of my water.

"No, I'm the one who should be sorry. I know I'm late. Too late. No excuses, other than dallying around outside, making like a chimney. I hope that doesn't bother you too much."

I shake my head. "Oh, not at all," I say, lying.

He opens his menu. "So what's good here?"

"You tell me. You're the professional."

"Yeah. This place is probably our main competition."

"Sheesh! I should have thought of that. This is the same old fare you see day in and day out. You're probably sick of meatloaf and hot turkey sandwiches." I meet his eyes. "You wanna go someplace else? There's that Thai place over on Mercer. Or that Mexican one down the street."

"It's okay." He smiles. "I like this kind of food. Especially on a night like tonight—chilly, damp." He peers down at the menu, running a finger over the offerings. Aside from the aforementioned meatloaf, there's chicken-fried steak, fish and chips, and chili. "It warms me up inside and out."

Big Red comes back. She winks at me and grins, gives me a little oh-so-subtle thumbs-up, barely raising her hand above table level. "What can I get you boys to drink? Something stronger than java, maybe?"

A beer sounds lovely. "A draft beer'd be awesome, whatever you have that leans toward an IPA."

"Gotcha." She turns to Jimmy.

"Just a Coke," he tells her.

"Coming right up." She walks away.

"Not a drinker?"

He shakes his head and smiles. "Nah. Not anymore. Smoking's about my only vice these days." He stares down at the table, then looks up at me, clearly a little sheepish. "I might as well put it right out there. I'm in recovery." He nods, although I'm not quite sure why. Nerves?

"That's cool. And probably strike number two for me, anyway?"

He raises his eyebrows. "Oh? Why's that?"

"It's bad enough I bring you to the same kind of place you work in every day. I also have to bring you to a joint that has the slogan, 'Alcoholics serving alcoholics since 1929.'"

That seems to tickle him, and we both laugh. When we stop, I ask, "Is it okay with you if I have a beer? I don't have to, you know. I can send it back."

He puts his hand back on mine, touching me for a second. "It's okay, Marc. Alcohol wasn't my problem anyway. Much. But I find it's best for me, right now, to stay away from any mind-altering substances." His expression goes dark and faraway for a bit. When he comes back, he asks, "Can we talk about something else? How was work today?"

"You don't want to hear about that. My title is communications specialist, but really it should just be administrative assistant. I get to do a bit of writing, but it's all about super dry stuff—government health-care contracts." I grin. "You want to hear more about that?"

He chuckles. "I guess not."

We keep things simple for the next few minutes. Talking about the weather. How we're both not from here—which is fairly common. I've never lived anywhere that seems to have so few hometown people.

We order. He gets a cheeseburger and fries, and I get the hot turkey sandwich, substituting the mashed potatoes with fries and gravy all over everything. Healthy! But so good.

After we've finished our meals, things get quiet. There are only a few people in the restaurant—an old man at the counter with a copy of the *Seattle Times* folded just so next to his plate. I haven't noticed the other gay couple leave yet, so I assume they're somewhere behind us. But there's a mood around us—kind of slow and serene. If I close my eyes, I can imagine hearing the rain coming down outside.

"It feels good," I let myself say. "Just being here with you." Heat rises to my face yet again, wondering if this is too much of a confession, like when you say "I love you" to a guy too quickly.

But Jimmy smiles. "It does. I'm pretty comfortable too." He reaches over to squeeze my hand again and then lets go. I like how he touches me. It's almost like he's reassuring me or, I don't know, reassuring himself that I'm here.

I push my plate away, amazed that I ate every last bite. "Why?"

"Why what?" He pushes his own plate away, and I can see why he's so lean. He only ate half his meal. All those fries going to waste. If it wasn't our first date, I'd be snatching them up.

"Why did you want to come out with me? I'm old enough to be your dad."

"Oh, you are not!" He kicks me under the table. "How old are you, anyway? Thirty-four? Thirty-five? Don't hit me if I'm guessing too old."

"I'm flattered. I'm sixty."

Jimmy's eyes widen.

I laugh. "You should see your face. I was kidding."

He gives a slow shake of his head. "If that were the case, I'd want to know your secret, because you would be remarkably, almost miraculously, well-preserved."

"I'll be forty in a few months."

Jimmy lets out a low whistle. "Wow. Ancient. Should I call you Pops?"

I smirk. "How old are you?" Do I really want to know?

"Twenty-three."

I nod. "See? I could be your dad."

"If you had me when you were, like, sixteen, I suppose."

"It's possible. I lost my virginity to a girl in my high school, right about at that age." I laugh. "I was confused. I remember it was in the front seat of my mom's car in the elementary school parking lot." I snicker. "If she'd gotten pregnant, here you'd be, calling me Pops."

"I'm not gonna call you Pops, or Daddy, or say that you look good for your age," Jimmy tells me. "You just look good, man." He smiles. "I'm not into ages. Older. Younger. In-between. It doesn't really matter." He winks. "I just like men."

"Me too. So we have something in common."

"Good thing to have in common," Jimmy says. "Especially for a couple of homos."

The conversation grinds to a halt. I don't want to leave, but the harder I try to think of something to say, the more elusive the perfect conversational gambit becomes. This is what happens to me. I've always been the quiet guy, Mr. Still Waters, the loner. The kind who prefers curling up with a good book to going out to a party.

Except for tonight. I want to be with Jimmy. Just looking at him makes me feel warm—yeah, there's lust there, but there's something more.

At an absolute loss, I finally push myself to ask what I think is a fairly innocent question. "So, what brought you to Seattle?"

He leans back in his seat, staring at me like he's thinking it over. "I could be a smartass and say a Greyhound. Which is the truth, but I don't think that's what you're asking." He sighs. "I needed to get away from home."

"Where's home?"

"Chester, West Virginia. Ever heard of it?"

I shake my head.

"I'm not surprised. It's only a couple thousand people. But..." He widens his eyes, like he's about to deliver the world's most delightful surprise. "They have the world's biggest teapot there."

"What?" The distinction is so weird it makes me laugh.

"Yeah, right on the main road coming into town. It's like a little house."

"Why?"

"It's pottery country, I guess. Homer Laughlin? The company that makes Fiestaware? Please tell me you've heard of that?"

I nod.

"It's made in the area."

We're quiet for a few minutes. Then Jimmy says, "I had to get out, for a lot of reasons. One, there's so little work in the area. It's pretty poor." He shrugs. "It's pretty, too, but that doesn't make up for the poverty. Rolling Appalachian foothills don't put food on the table. And you wouldn't want to drink the water out of the Ohio River."

"So you just up and came to Seattle?"

"Yup. I'd just gotten laid off from my job as a greeter at the Walmart across the river and thought...why not? I liked Kurt Cobain's music. I was a fan of *Grey's Anatomy*."

"Both excellent reasons to move to the Emerald City. And that brought you all the way across the country?"

"Well, those and wanting to get as far away as possible from my crazy-ass mother."

Now we're getting somewhere, I thought.

"Oh, I have one of those myself," I say, not because it's true, but to be agreeable and to get Jimmy to continue talking, to spill his personal beans.

"I don't want to get into a crazy mom contest." Jimmy looks toward the counter, where Big Red is mixing up a milkshake for a guy in sweats and a camo jacket who's just come in and seated himself on one of the stools. There's something winsome and also very sad in Jimmy's expression.

"It's okay. We can talk about something else."

"Nah. You should know what you're dealing with before you go any further." Jimmy turns back to me, eyeing me like it's a challenge. "My mom was a drunk. She was a brilliant woman—at one time. She even taught French at Kent State, which wasn't too far away. But then she met my dad."

"Was he crazy too?"

Jimmy blew out a breath of air. "You don't know the half of it! I'm gonna need a cigarette if I'm gonna tell you my life story. You wanna book? Get out of here?"

I hadn't considered much beyond the present. I didn't know if I was ready for a my-place-or-yours moment.

He must have read my mind. "We don't have to go anywhere in particular. We can just walk around a bit."

"But it's raining."

"Yeah. And you're a Seattleite now. You don't let the rain slow you down. Don't tell me you own an umbrella." He grins, and I think how cute it is—the way his lips turn up at one corner, kind of lopsided. I have a moment of déjà vu, like he reminds me of someone. It passes.

"You're right." I give a little nod to Big Red, who scurries over to the table. Before Jimmy has a chance to protest, I hand her my card. "Can you ring us up?"

*

Outside, we wander around for a while, silent, enjoying the rain. It's slowed now to a gentle mist, and it feels good, actually, once you get past the initial shock of the chill. I'm stunned when Jimmy reaches over and takes my hand, intertwining my fingers with his.

I glance at him, sure my surprise is obvious.

"It's cool," he says. "No one cares." He smiles. "Except me."

I squeeze his hand for a moment and let our two palms continue their first kiss. Even though Seattle's a very liberal and progressive city, there are still things like gay-bashings here, so I can't help but feel a little concerned. I'm not used to public displays of affection, and I look around guardedly before I tell myself to cut it out. We have just as much right as anyone else on a first date to hold hands. And if someone has a problem with it, well, that's *their* problem.

Besides, there aren't many other people out and about right now.

I try to relax, to let go of my worry and apprehension. I remind myself how much I like the warmth and touch of this cute guy beside me.

At last we come to a little bar just at the base of Queen Anne Hill. It's called Lily's. Unpretentious, it has a white brick front with a large glass picture window. The glass is tinted, so we can't see inside. A big awning covers a patio, underneath which are grouped about a half dozen tables. With the rain and the chill in the air, no one's sitting at any of them. I think of grabbing one of those tables, since we're already chilled and damp, and Jimmy can tell me more about his crazy-ass mom and growing up in a town that has as its claim to fame, the world's largest teakettle. But it's a bar, and I don't want to make Jimmy uncomfortable again.

I continue moving, but he pulls me back. "Want to stop here?"

I slow my pace. "Are you sure?" I look up and down the front of Lily's. The door opens, and a patron comes out, an older woman with long gray hair and a bright yellow rain slicker. When she opens the door, she releases the sound of voices and laughter from inside, along with Adele singing "Rolling in the Deep." She smiles at us and then moves off into the rain, head down.

Jimmy shrugs. "Why not? We could be really adventurous and grab one of those tables over yonder." He nods at the outdoor seating. "Show we're die-hard Seattleites."

"I just meant...it's a bar and you're—"

"In recovery," he finishes for me. "I know. But it's cool. As I told you before, alcohol's not my problem."

It would be the perfect time to ask him what *was* his problem—or should it be what *is*?—since the old wisdom goes that you're never fully cured of any kind of addiction, only recovering. But I'm hesitant. The moment seems imbued with a kind of magic. The streets of this busy neighborhood are quiet, and I don't think it's because of a little rain or it being a weeknight. I have the fanciful notion that the world's stepped aside so we two can get better acquainted.

"Is it a gay bar?" I whisper.

He leans close and whispers back, "I don't know. Does it need to be?"

Again, I'm struck—and maybe a little dismayed—by how conservative I am. Why do I think two gay men on a first date even need to know their place and be in a gay bar? So we're more comfortable? God, I hope we, as a society, are beginning to put such thoughts behind us.

"Not at all."

We step under the awning and search out the perfect table. The one near the wall, just past the picture window, kind of beckons. It has a corner of the building on one side, plus the front, and it looks cozy. I point to it. "How about that one?"

"You read my mind." He starts toward the table.

"Uh, grab a seat. I'll go in and get us a couple of drinks and let someone know we're out here. What'll you have?"

Jimmy sits down and calls over, "A shot of tequila with a Stella Artois back." He grins, and even in the dark, I see the mischievous little boy lurking within the man.

"Right." I turn to the door and start to pull it open to see if he stops me.

"A Coke!" he yells just before I head inside.

At the bar I order two Cokes. I still don't feel right about drinking in front of him, even if alcohol isn't his poison of choice.

He eyes my drink when I come back. "Tell me that's a rum and Coke."

"Nope. Same as you."

"You don't have to do that, man."

I put my hand over his. "A Coke sounded good." I take a sip. "Damn!" I close my eyes in ecstasy for a second.

"What?"

"I'd forgot how good the full-sugar stuff tastes. I gave it up for diet a long time ago. I don't think I've had fully leaded for years."

"I can't stand diet stuff. When someone asks me if I have a sweet tooth, I always say no. Then I tell them I have sweet teeth—all of them."

We laugh together and grow quiet for a while. The rain is coming down a bit harder now, and it's nice—a gentle, rhythmic patter on the canvas above.

"So you were telling me about your family."

"Yeah, there really isn't that much to tell. They were both smart, insanely so. Like Mensa smart. But they threw it all away on..." he trailed off, then picked up with "Bad habits. Mom wasn't too awful, not at first. When I was born, she was a hotshot young professor of French literature on a tenure track at Kent. She used to read me *The Little Prince* in French when I was a kid. She wanted me to be bilingual."

"And are you?"

He shakes his head. "That didn't last long."

I cock my head but don't say a word, encouraging him to go on, letting him know I'm listening.

He takes a sip of his Coke. "I never did drink," he says. "Not even when I was a kid and my buddies were sneaking beers and stronger stuff out of their mom and dad's liquor cabinets. I'd seen too fast and too early what booze can do to a family." He looked away. "It basically robbed me of my parents.

"They drank together—it was what they did for fun on the weekends. Except it didn't take long for them to smack their heads and wonder, why not bring the fun into Monday? Tuesday? Wednesday? And so on and so forth. Meanwhile, Dad indulged other fun pastimes, like gambling at the racetrack near us, smoking weed, and chasing women. That last one was what eventually split them up. I grew up most of my childhood with just my mom.

"She never got over my dad leaving her. She knew about the cheating all along and could put up with it as long as he came home every night. She had this devotion to him I'll never understand. I mean, the man was gorgeous—in a movie star way." He smiled, but it was a sad smile. "The closest comparison I can make for him is George Clooney?" He looks at me.

I nod.

"Yeah, Mom knew about his infidelities. She had the attitude of not caring where he got his tires pumped as long as he came home to ride."

Jimmy sighs. "But then, I guess it wasn't about sex anymore. He met this young woman at Kent State, an undergraduate, maybe even a freshman. The complete opposite of my mom—all blonde and WASPy. And she didn't drink, didn't smoke, and was a total Christian." He shakes his head. "They've been married for over a dozen years now. Dad's a deacon at their church, and I have three little half brothers that I don't even know."

"I'm sorry."

He waves my consolation away. "Ah, it's okay. Dad leaving us was hard, but what happened after he left was harder." He leans forward. "You sure you want to hear this?"

"I do."

Jimmy takes a deep breath, like he's about to plunge into even deeper waters. And I suppose he is.

Jimmy closes his eyes for a moment. Then he opens them to take a sip of his drink. The expression on his face is faraway as he stares out at the rain. I suspect he's gone somewhere else.

"You want to hear a story?" he asks, not looking at me. He doesn't wait for me to answer either. "Picture a little eight-year-old boy, cute as a button, with reddish-brown hair, a pug nose, and freckles. There's a bit of the devil about him. But he's a good kid.

"It's Christmas Eve, and him and his mom are at least warm in their trailer. The wind howls outside, shaking the mobile home on the cinder blocks that pass for a foundation. Over the quilt-covered couch, the picture window looks out on snow—coming down hard.

"There are no Christmas carols playing. Other than the wind, there's only the sound of applause and cheering as yet another game show unspools before us on our portable TV.

"Mom's already half in the bag." He stops, looks over at me, and I think he's testing how I'm taking in his story. "No. Make that fully in the bag. One hundred percent shitfaced. She's had her Christmas cheer, the same Christmas cheer she's been having during the holidays, plus spring, summer, and fall. Vodka. She used to like good stuff like Stoli, but these days it's bottom-of-the-shelf crap that's a step up from grain alcohol. She's snoring, leaning half over the edge of the couch.

"The little guy plucks a cigarette, burned down to the filter, out from between her fingers and places the butt in an overflowing ashtray on the coffee table.

"He looks at his ma and whispers, "It's Christmas Eve, Mom." She doesn't stir. He wonders if maybe she's dreaming of sugar plum fairies. He sits beside her and lays his head gently on her arm. The fabric of her pink quilted housecoat is soft against his skin. She smells of cigarettes, alcohol, and a faint aroma of Jean Nate, which she uses in her bathwater. *Is Daddy coming home for Christmas?* he wonders. He barely says the words aloud because a part of him knows how stupid it would be to wake her. He's learned from past experience that rousing his drunk mother doesn't always work out for the best. She's been known to slap his face, which is preferable to the alternative—a cold stare and a retreat into her bedroom at the back of the trailer with a slam of her door.

"But there's this part of him, see? This part that's part sad, part mad that it's fuckin' Christmas Eve and he's sitting here with her and she's passed out drunk. There's no tree, no presents, not even the fuckin' Grinch or something on TV. So he asks again, louder, "Is Daddy coming home for Christmas?" He knows the answer, but he's mad and getting madder. He keeps repeating the question over and over, louder each time, until he's screaming the words, not even aware anymore of the TV or even his mother's presence in the room. He's kind of lost in a void where he's a victim and feels justified in screaming because life is unfair.

"He doesn't even notice his mom wake up. It's in the middle of a scream that he looks over and sees her staring at him, her mouth open. It's weird. She looks like she doesn't even recognize him.

"Finally she comes back to herself. She leans forward to grab a cigarette out of the pack on the coffee table. She lights it and picks up the remote to begin a little channel surfing. "Go to bed," she tells him, not taking her eyes from the screen.

"He listens because he's a good boy.

"But later, in the middle of the night, he dreams of hoofbeats on the roof of the trailer and wakes up in the dark. He lies still for a minute, still in the web of the magic his dream cast. And then it all comes back to him—his reality.

"The TV's still playing in the living room. He creeps from his closet-sized bedroom and stands beside the couch. His mom's stretched out on her back, mouth open, snoring like a lumberjack. Ash covers the front of her robe, and drool runs from the corner of her mouth.

"Not a pretty picture. But this is his mom, right? And he loves her.

"He gets an idea. He wants to give her Christmas. So he goes into the kitchen. One edge of their counter has a stack of newspapers. His mom gets the little local rag on weekdays and the big Pittsburgh paper on Sundays. He pulls the funnies out from the Sunday paper and then tiptoes by his mom, headed for her room. Even then, he's wise enough to wonder why he bothers with the tippy-toes. He could march through in steel-toed boots with the high school marching band, and she wouldn't wake up. He could drive a Mack truck through.

"In her bedroom, he goes through her drawers. He finds an old bracelet made of silver and garnets—her birthstone—she used to wear. He wraps it up in a sheet of comics, tucking the edges around to secure it. He finds other things—a maroon sweater, soft as a bird, a book called *I Know Why the Caged Bird Sings*, a cassette tape of someone named Bonnie Raitt, and an old jar of bath salts. He wraps all of these things in the funny papers, smiling, removed for a while from the little trailer, just thinking about making Christmas."

Won't Mom be surprised in the morning?

"He takes his gifts and sets them at the foot of the coat rack by the front door. It's no Christmas tree, but it'll have to do.

"He goes back to bed. He lies there, too excited to sleep, until the gray light of dawn creeps in through his blinds. He hears Mom moving around at last, and he can barely contain his excitement. He forces himself to lie still, listening to the tearing of papers.

"And finally he creeps from his room. His mom sits on the floor, her presents scattered around her. When she looks up at him, her face is wet with tears. She doesn't say anything, just holds her arms out to him.

"He goes to her and lets himself be held. He can't remember the last time she hugged him, and this hug, this squeeze so hard it hurts a little, is all the Christmas he needs."

Jimmy stares down at the table. I admit, I'm a little choked up. A couple of tears have leaked out and run down my face. I don't know what to say.

He looks over at me, searching, I suppose, for my reaction.

I get up and move toward him. I reach down and place my hands under his arms to raise him up. I gather him in my arms and I kiss him, deeply, heedless of who might be scurrying by, losing myself in his trembling warmth as the rain patters down above us.

Wednesday

Chapter Seven

JIMMY

I open my eyes to darkness, a boom of thunder, a flash of lightning, and a question.

Why?

Why did I open myself up like that? Why did I tell him so much stuff about my childhood? About my mom? And God, that Christmas!

Was I trying to play on his sympathy? Trying to build up a foundation to make it easier for Marc when he eventually remembers? When he knows the truth of who I am and what I did to him? Was the reason selfish? Just wanting to be seen in a pitiable light? Was I thinking that maybe by doing so, he'd come to love me? To think *Oh the poor guy—he's had it rough?*

I turn over in my bed and grab my phone off the stack of books I use for a nightstand. I hit the Home button and the screen illuminates. It's a little after 3:00 a.m. Another flash of lightning lights up my small room with silver light, making it appear to be a sad set from some old black-and-white movie.

A grumble of thunder follows, and I think it's strange. Where I grew up, in West Virginia, thunder and lightning were common, especially in the summer months, when we could endure some pretty wicked storms. Seattle doesn't have that so much—even though it's a city famous for its rain. Here precipitation is gentler, a little more understated—gray skies, drizzle, mists. Downpours happen, but not as often. And thunder and lightning? In the winter? Almost unheard of.

I wonder if the weather is a reflection somehow of my inner turmoil.

I sigh and try to relax back into my pillow, which smells vaguely of my sweat. My eyes have adjusted a bit to the darkness, so the room takes on gray tones. I stare up at the ceiling, tracing with my eyes a hairline crack that runs from the old cut-glass light fixture to a corner. I think a spider crawls along it, using the crack as a marker.

But that could just be my imagination.

I attempt to stop myself from wondering why I opened myself up so much to Marc the night before. Maybe it was just because I wanted to. Maybe it was simply because I wanted him to know me, to see the parts of me that were vulnerable.

Maybe I just want, at last, finally, to make myself vulnerable to another person, to hand over for a moment the weight I carry around.

To be *seen*.

Deep thoughts, mister, for three-o-fuckin-clock in the morning!

Yet I could see something in his eyes as I talked. There was more than sympathy there, but a need to share the burden, a desire, maybe, to know me, the real me, more intimately.

I turn over in bed, eye the pack of smokes. I know there's only a couple left, but now that my focus is on them, I can't resist. Feeling like my head weighs a ton, I force myself to sit up.

Kevin made me promise when I moved in that I'd always take my smoking outside, and I always have. But it's late, and my legs feel like lead flows through them. It's not so much that it's raining outside that deters me, that tempts me to break the rule. It's the whole thought of getting dressed, making my way through my bedroom, the living room, the front hallway, and the vestibule that stops me. It seems like a journey of a thousand miles.

I grab my lighter and one of my last smokes and take them over to the sole window. I lift it, letting in the fresh-washed smell of the air, with just a tinge of salt from the Sound a few blocks away. Seems a shame to pollute it.

I squat in my boxers by the window and light up. The nicotine hits, and already, with just that first puff, I feel calmer. Someday I'm gonna have to confront this addiction. But not yet.

I take another drag.

Maybe I told him all that so I could get to *the kiss*. I close my eyes, savoring the memory of what just might go down as the best kiss of my life. And, as a guy whose lips have been smashed up against the lips of more men than he'd care to mention, that's saying a lot.

It was like rest at the end of a long journey.

It was like weight being lifted from my shoulders.

It was like a magical reward for allowing myself to be open and vulnerable.

Even I didn't know, at the end of my tale of holiday woe, a kiss would be exactly what I needed to put a bandage on my pain, to demonstrate that someone had finally, finally, finally listened to me and understood.

But Marc knew. He understood when I finished pouring out a story I'd never told anyone before—one that, for sure, I had hardly ever even allowed myself to confront—what I needed was a kiss.

And not just any kiss—but one filled with electricity, passion, and best of all, comfort.

I shake my head, remembering and staring out at the rain-slicked street below me. That kiss must have lasted for five minutes, maybe more. It was like our two bodies melded together, became one. Believe it or not, that kiss was better than any sex I'd ever had.

Is that even possible?

It was. Trust me.

I think we only broke apart because we heard the door to the bar squeak open and a cough. We broke apart like two guilty kids, grinning sheepishly at the guy with the salt-and-pepper beard who'd emerged.

I don't think he even noticed us. He was too intent on lighting up his cigarette, a need I know only too well.

I look down at my own smoke, burned now almost to the filter, and think about using the cherry at its tip to light the last one in the pack. That would be so indulgent, so wasteful. Smoking, besides being filthy and unhealthy, is also something I can't really afford.

Anyway, the guy, a fellow addict, really didn't pay us any mind as he smoked, surveying the traffic going by, the waxing and waning of the rain.

Marc smiled sheepishly at me. "Busted."

I shrugged. "Not really. I don't think he even knows we're here."

The man turned to us. "I know." And then he turned away again.

We smiled at each other and simply gazed into each other's eyes. I held his hand under the table, squeezing it, feeling its warmth. I wanted so much to kiss him again.

Marc said those dreadful words after a long period of blissful silence. "We should go. I have work in the morning."

I nodded, sad. "I do too. Probably earlier than you. I open tomorrow, which means I need to be there no later than six thirty."

I wanted to say, "Take me home." I wanted to say, "I don't want to split up, not now, not ever." I wanted to say, "Even that first time we met, the one you don't remember, I think I felt the same. And that's my particular pain to bear, because a stupid drug and how it obliterated every part of me that's good caused me to do stupid little things that, if you remember, you'll hate me for…"

I remember I forced myself not to go down that road. Not then. Things were too perfect. *For just one night, Lord, let me have perfect.*

And as we got up from the table and headed out into the night, it was. Perfect. We held hands all the way to his bus stop, where we shared another kiss. Shorter, but no less intense.

I left Marc standing on the corner with a promise that we'd see each other again. Soon.

Is tonight too soon?

I stand up, grind out my smoke in the ashtray on the dresser. I leave the window open and crawl back into bed, thinking I can squeeze in a couple more hours sleep.

Maybe I'll dream of Marc.

And when I wake and the hour becomes decent, I'll text him. Is tonight too soon?

*

Turns out I didn't need to text him, because when I woke up, a text from him was already waiting for me.

If you can stand being with me two nights in a row, I'd love to see you again tonight. Maybe someplace more private. Deal?

I stare down at the screen, smiling. *Oh, honey, it's a deal*, I think, and then text my enthusiastic yes. I text him my address, tell him I'll cook him dinner. I'm not bad in that department, you know.

*

Later, once I get home from work in the afternoon, Kevin's waiting for me. He looks up from whatever he's watching on TV. There's a look of annoyance on his face. "You smoked in the house," he says.

"Hello to you too," I say. "Have a good day?"

He shuts off the TV with the remote. I think he was watching *The People's Court*. He gives a little yip that I suppose is meant to be a laugh.

"And I'm sorry. It was only one. I couldn't sleep."

"Only one? C'mon, bud, you're enough of an addict to know that 'only one' is never an excuse."

Damn. I'm excited about getting ready for my date, and here's my roomie, harshing my perfectly natural buzz. I take in a couple of deep breaths to calm myself. This is a small practice I never would have done once upon a time. No, once upon a time I would have reacted with rage, jumped all over Kevin, told him how unfair he was and if he had a problem with my smoking in the house, he could shove it up his ass, just for something different to put up there. The old me would have lit a cigarette up right then and there just to show him who's who and what's what.

But I'm not that guy anymore. I wait a few seconds, still breathing deeply, resisting the urge to ask him how he could even smell anything when I left the window open all night. "You're right. You want me to pick up some Febreze next time I'm at Bartell's?"

He shakes his head. "What I want you to do is not smoke in your room."

"Done," I say. "You can go back to your TV now."

He points the remote at the TV and presses the power button. Marilyn Milian is shouting something in Spanish, something about the cheap coming out expensive.

As I head toward my room, he calls out, "I thought maybe we could order a pizza tonight. I have a coupon for Pagliacci. You pick the toppings."

I stop in my tracks. This is unusual for Kevin, and if I didn't have the plans I did, I would have bent over backward to join him. I turn back. "Sorry. I have a date tonight." I sit back down. "And here's the thing. I invited him to come over."

"And what? You want a three-way?" he snorts.

"No, but tonight would be an excellent time to—"

"Make myself scarce?"

"Well, I wouldn't put it that way."

"I would," Kevin says. He frowns, and I wonder if I'm going to have to just accept that he'll be here in his room, or worse, on the couch with the TV on. "But don't worry. I was planning on going to a meeting tonight, anyway. The one over in Green Lake? We usually go out for coffee after, so the place'll be all yours. So you can get up to whatever shenanigans you have in mind. Just stay off my bed." He grins.

"Thanks. I don't know about shenanigans, but I'm gonna cook for him."

"Cook? Whoa!" He laughs. "Who's the lucky fella tonight? Someone new? Yet another hopeful from the diner?"

"It's the same guy from last night. Marc."

Kevin's mouth drops open. "Two nights in a row? And the same guy? And you're gonna make him dinner?" He looks me up and down. "Are you sure you're my roommate?"

"C'mon, Kev."

"Oh, don't give me that. I don't think I've ever seen you with the same guy twice."

He has a point. Back in my Tina days, that was just par for the course, because one, or a dozen, could never satisfy. That was the thing with Tina—you could have multiple partners and gang bangs all night, and you *still* wouldn't be satisfied. Because there was no such thing as *satisfied*. You had desire out the wazoo—literally—and no way to ever feel like you'd had enough. It was sick. Like being thirsty and having access to gallons and gallons of water, but after each swallow, you looked around for more.

But even lately, even after two years sober, I confess that I've never met a guy like Marc, one I want to see again.

A shiver passes through me, like somebody just traipsed across my grave. I recognize the feeling as something bad. What's the word? *Foreboding?*

I sit on the couch, wishing I could light up. "You're right. You're right. But this guy is special."

"You really like him?"

I nod.

"Good sex?"

I shake my head. "We never got there. Just a couple of amazing kisses." I grin, both pleased to let Kevin know this relatively new aspect of myself *and* at the memory.

He gets up from his chair and comes over to me. He lifts up some of my hair to inspect my scalp. He pushes me forward, yanking my shirt collar back so he can peer down my neck. I flinch away. "What the hell are you doing?"

He snickers. "Checking to see if I can find the signs of the pod. You know, the one they left behind and that you hatched out of—when they took the real Jimmy." He sits back down.

"It's me. Maybe it's just the right time for me to meet the right guy." And then I recall my original night with Marc, a little over two years ago, and my heart plummets. My mind tells me *This ain't never gonna work. Find somebody else before this all blows up in your face.*

And speaking of faces, I see Marc's again in my mind's eye, and my body responds with all kinds of warmth—sexual heat and a kind of weird feeling that simply to be close to him is enough.

I can't let him go.

But can I just go on with this masquerade? Doesn't he deserve to know who I really am?

I eye Kevin, who's turned the TV back on and is now caught up in a *People's Court* case involving a Pomeranian mauling a pit bull.

He's my roommate, not my confessor. He's a nice enough man, a little weird, but then, aren't we all?

Not wanting him to know is what my reticence really boils down to. He knows I'm an addict, and that's enough for right now. He doesn't need all the sordid details. I know he wouldn't judge me for the things I've done, but still, there could be a shift. He might lock his shit up more securely, for example. Never leave his wallet lying around.

There's only one person I can really share this with. Someone who will listen. Someone who won't judge— really. Someone who's both been there and been there *for me.*

Miriam.

I wish I had time to get over to the east side, where she lives, even if it was just for a quick cup of coffee, but I don't. Marc'll be here by six thirty.

I stand and then grope around in my pockets. I pull out my pack of Marlboro Blacks and show them to Kevin. "See? I'm taking these outside. I'll be on the front stoop. Enjoy your show."

"Enjoy polluting yourself!" he calls just as I'm closing the front door. As an added kick in the pants, he coughs dramatically. I roll my eyes.

See what I mean? I can't tell him stuff like what I need to tell Miriam.

I get outside and plop down. Our building has a wide set of cement stairs at its front, and they're ideal for sitting on, having a smoke, and watching the world go by. I'm not the only resident of the building who often has this same idea, so I'm grateful to be alone.

I'm also thankful there's no rain, at least not right now. The sky's already dark, and there's damp in the air, but nothing is falling from the sky. In Seattle, we call this nice weather. Plus it's almost fifty degrees, which means I can do without my denim jacket.

I watch the traffic go by for a few minutes. Light up a smoke. I'm stalling.

Finally I pull my phone from my pocket, bring Miriam up. My finger hovers over her picture. She has the sweetest face, the kindest smile. I know her hair is dyed and that she's had a nose job, but genuine warmth and kindness radiate from this pic, which I took the last time I saw her. We'd had lunch on my birthday in the International District. She'd treated me to pho and had given me a leather strap bracelet I still wear—and cherish. I press the screen.

"Hey, sweetie." Her voice in my ear immediately relaxes me, makes me feel hugged.

"Hey yourself."

"How's tricks? Everything going well? I was just about to start making supper. Adobo chicken and roasted cauliflower. Chocolate pudding for dessert. Homemade."

"Wow. Fancy. Can I come?"

"Why, sure you can! We're eating at seven."

I laugh. "You're so nice. But I can't, not tonight, good as all that stuff sounds. I have a date." And that reminds me that I haven't even thought what I'll make for Marc, and most likely, I'll have to get myself out to the store.

"Oh, honey, that's great. Same guy?"

I nod and then realize she can't see me. "Yup. Marc. I told you about him."

"Yeah, you were nervous about seeing him. Something about having already met? Did you guys hang? Was it wonderful?"

"It was magical, Miriam."

"Aw! That's so sweet. Tell me all about it."

I let her in on the details of our date—the sharing, the kiss, the bliss. The rain. It's all such a sweet memory. Even though it was only yesterday, it has all the earmarks of a very nice dream. My heart starts to beat a little harder as I think about spoiling the fluffy and feel-good ambiance of the dream with stark reality.

Maybe I should just keep things to myself? I immediately reject that idea. Secrets are not what my life in recovery is about. Rigorous honesty is what the twelve-step program demands.

"Wow," Miriam gushes. "That sounds really romantic. Like something out of a movie."

I nod again, ignoring the futility of it. I light another cigarette from the butt of the last. "There's, uh, something I want to talk to you about. About Marc and me. There's a little trouble in paradise, see?" I expect her to chuckle, but she doesn't. "You got a few minutes?"

I hear the scrape of a chair being pulled out. "Sweetie, I have all the minutes in the world. For you."

"You sure? You said you were making supper."

"I said I was getting ready to. I have time. And you're just stalling. Tell me what's going on."

I'm quiet for a long while—so long, she prods me.

"Go ahead."

Little flashes come to me, like quick cuts from a movie. They turn my stomach, but they keep coming anyway.

There I am in a filthy motel room in Tukwila, not far from Sea-Tac Airport, everything in the world I own now strewn across the floor and the bed. It stinks in there of fast food, cigarettes, and sweat. I'm at the small table by the window, curtains shut, eyes glued to the screen of my laptop, on a hookup site. I scan restlessly through the images—looking for someone cute, someone vulnerable, someone who'd be stupid enough to invite a weasel like me into his home.

You'd be surprised.

There's me a few minutes into a conversation I'm having with this guy up on the north side. I have my arm tied up, pressing the moist flesh restlessly for a vein. They roll away from me like spaghetti under my skin. It's frustrating. But as I always manage to, I find a good one. I bite off the orange plastic cap on the syringe I've got loaded up with a hefty dose of liquefied Tina. I poke the needle into the vein and draw out a little blood to make sure I've hit pay dirt. The blood swirls, calming, a celebration, releasing in me a huge anticipatory surge. I have to remind myself to breathe. It's like when you're at the very peak of the first summit on a roller coaster. I know I'm not going to make the mistake of injecting the drug under my skin, as I've done before, causing an abscess, but right into a vein. Suddenly the world is all about what's getting ready to hit...

I plunge the top of the syringe down, flooding my veins with Tina. Immediately the drug courses through and my body fills with golden heat. It feels like liquid fire. Sunlight pulses through my veins. Sweat pops out all over, trickles down my face, my spine. I hear a chorus of a thousand angels singing.

This is it.

This is what I threw my whole life away for.

This is all I care about.

I close my eyes, undo the clasp around my upper arm, and pant a little. My dick gets hard.

This is wonderful, a one-way ticket to heaven...

"Honey?" Miriam jars me out of the reverie. It's scary how fast I can go back there, to that time. I can almost feel the searing, delicious heat in my veins.

I want to do it again.

I want to puke.

"You wanted to tell me something?"

"Yeah," I say quietly. "I wanted to tell you that I've met Marc before."

"You said that."

"But listen. It was two years ago. I was living in some dive out by the airport because I'd lost my job, lost my apartment, lost everyone close to me."

"There but for the grace of God," Miriam says, and I know she means it.

"I've told you I did some dealing?"

"Yes."

"And that sometimes I stole from people?"

"Uh-huh. Go on…"

I take in a deep breath and blow it out. "You won't hate me for—"

She cuts me off. "I won't hate you for *anything*. Sweetheart, there's nothing you can say that's gonna shock me. And better, there's nothing you can say that's gonna change my opinion of you."

"Remind me what that opinion is again?"

She laughs. "That you're a good guy. That you *are* love. And *loved*. And that you've made mistakes, but they were steps on the path of your journey. You *needed* to get high. You *needed* to do the things you consider bad.

"Why? Because you learned from them. Because you *grew*." She draws in a breath and lets it out slowly. "Sometimes, the worst things we did were actually the best because they taught us so much."

I pause to let her words, her counsel, sink in. I know she's right. Still, it's hard to tell her the truth.

"This guy, Marc? We hooked up back then. I, uh, got him to invite me over. I went to his place, high as a kite, and I fucked him. But that's not the problem. He made that choice. But he didn't make the choice for the other things I did to him."

"Tell me."

"Every time he left the room—and I stayed all night with him—I'd get up and go through his things. His drawers, his gym bag on the floor, his closet, a jewelry box. And I took whatever I could get my hands on—watches, electronics, earbuds, cash—basically anything I could turn over quickly so I'd have enough to one, keep getting high, and two, keep a roof over my head, shoddy as it was."

"And he never knew?"

"I'm sure he did. When I got out of there at dawn, though, I don't think he had any idea. And to make sure he couldn't bug me anymore, I blocked him on my phone and on the site where we met." I stare down at the damp concrete of the stairs below me. A car goes by, its tires hissing on the wet pavement. "It was my MO back then."

"You were a different person. And now you're worried that—what? He'll recognize you?"

"I don't know. I do look like a different person." I remind her about the dreads I used to have, the septum piercing. How skinny I was. I know it's very possible he might never put two and two together, and I tell Miriam that. "But I don't know if it's healthy or wise to live with a lie like that between us."

"It's not," Miriam says simply. "Lies fester. They get under the skin of a relationship. You want to be intimate with this guy? And I'm not talking about between the sheets, but truly intimate? You can't with a lie like that between you."

"So what are you saying?" I stand up, nerves suddenly jangling. It's like there's been a shot of adrenaline straight to my heart, and it's making me feel both giddy and sick. "I should call it off?"

"No, honey. I'm saying that somewhere down the road, if he doesn't figure it out, you'll need to have a talk with him."

"But when?"

"That'll come clear. You'll see."

"What should I do about tonight?" Part of me wants her to tell me to call it off, to go to a meeting, to rethink things. If I'm this mixed up and afraid, maybe I should take a step back. The thought of doing that, though, is a paradoxical relief and a terror.

But she doesn't. "Well, seems to me you have two choices."

"Keep things on or call them off?"

"No! Will you stop being so negative? So hard on yourself? The two choices you have, to me, are you can either worry about tonight or...not. You can get yourself all worked up with fear and anxiety, imagining the worst possible outcome. And working up that mental energy will probably give you just what you're worrying about. You'll have a shitty time."

"Miriam!"

She laughs. "I know, I don't curse. Unless it's necessary. And it was...and is.

"The second choice you have is to be excited about tonight. What will you make? Will he like it? Will that same magic come back when you kiss? Will the magic deepen? Will you get to second base? Third?" She snickers. "You can draw good energy tonight by *anticipating* it."

"Really, Miriam?" I have an urge to play devil's advocate. "Either way, it won't change how things shake out. What's gonna happen is gonna happen."

"Well, mister, I believe that how you think about things *will* shape them, but even if that isn't true, what do you have to lose by putting your focus on a positive outcome? Worrying isn't going to make things better, so you might as well be giddy with anticipation, and then at least you'll be in a better mood when you open that door."

She's right. I can't change what's going to occur by worrying. "Thanks, Miriam. You're a lifesaver. And a sage."

"Ah, get out of here. If that were true, maybe I could have avoided making some of the mistakes I did."

"Shhh." I try to silence her. "You know I love you. And I don't know what I'd do without you."

"I know what you'd do."

"What?"

"You'd get yourself to a grocery store pronto, because if I know you, all you have in the house is spoiled milk and some microwavable dinners. Maybe a bag of Doritos."

She's right, eerily so. But I won't give her the satisfaction. "Now who's being negative? It just might surprise you to know there's lettuce in the crisper, tomatoes on the counter, a couple of nice pieces of cod in the fridge, along with a delicious bottle of sparkling cider."

"Well, good for you! Speaking of dinner, I need to get busy rattling some pots and pans!"

"And so do I," I say but know I need to get myself to the store. At least the menu's planned...

*

Marc is prompt, arriving at 6:25. When I open the door, the sight of him nearly takes my breath away. Have you ever had that sensation? Just the sight of someone being a spark for joy? Just their very nearness ringing an alarm bell? It's like that for me.

He's wearing a pink Oxford button-down he's paired with a navy blue vest and gray cords. He looks fresh-scrubbed and optimistic. His smile is a beaming beacon, illuminating my heart.

He looks, quite simply, *delicious*. Never mind what we're going to have for dinner.

In the short time between my call to Miriam and right now, I've managed to get a lot accomplished. I've been to the grocery store, and inspired by the fib I told Miriam, I picked up a couple of nice black cod filets and the makings of a salad—a cucumber, some grape tomatoes, a red onion, and a bag of baby romaine, already washed. I bought a bottle of an Italian vinaigrette to dress it with. The fish is already waiting on a plate on the counter. I'll just salt and pepper it, then fry it up in a little butter and olive oil and serve it with lemon.

It doesn't matter what we eat anyway. Dessert is what's on my mind, especially now that I've gotten a glimpse of this man. Irrational as it is, I not only lust for him—that's the rational part; he's a DILF, as the kids say today—but I also believe I'm in love with him.

It's hopeless in so many ways.

But I let my fears of our prior association flutter out the kitchen window, which is permanently open because when they painted in here, they did it with the window open and neither Kevin nor I could ever get it to close.

We kiss, and yup, the magic from last night is still there. It's like a line of silken electricity connects our bodies. The kiss lasts much longer than a greeting normally would. Before I know it, our tongues are dueling and our hands are running up and down each other's backs, exploring, pulling closer. Our breathing gets heavy. I have to restrain myself from grabbing his ass. Oh, why restrain? I grab his ass and squeeze. The action sends a wave of blood straight into my dick, which immediately becomes rock hard.

He pulls away slightly and looks down. I have on only a pair of jersey camo shorts, and my dick juts out like a tent.

Marc laughs a little, but I'm flattered to see that bald hunger in his dark eyes as he takes in my erection. "Happy to see me?" he whispers.

I nod and pull him close, real close, so I can rub against him a bit. I feel a tremor course through me and realize I'm *this close* to coming. That will not do!

I force myself, hard as it is—pun intended—to pull away. "If we keep that up, I'm going to pull you right into bed."

Marc sighs, and I look down to see our kissing has had the same effect on him. I grin. "And the problem with that is?"

I touch his cheek and stare into his eyes for a moment before I say, "I want to make you a nice dinner." I chuckle. "*First*. I deliberately did not pick up anything for dessert." What he doesn't realize, I'm thinking, is how very important this is to me. I remember the drug-filled and—for me—lust-filled night we spent together two years ago and how it was all about being a nasty pig. Not that there's anything wrong with that! But when one of the people is fucking the other and casting an appraising glance around the bedroom, cataloging contents based on what to steal, what would be good to fence, well, it's a memory I wish I could just cut right out of my brain. When one of the people is so high he's unable to come, while the other person gets off within a half hour or so, there's an imbalance.

I want tonight to be *normal*. I want tonight to be *sweet*.

Is that so bad? I mean, I know we're both horny as hell, and we both would have no problem jumping between my sheets—and yes, I changed 'em earlier. But it's been so long since I've had a normal date with a guy. It's been forever—if ever—since I've welcomed real romance into my life. I want that. I want it now.

I push him gently toward the living room. "You go in and sit. I'll bring you a glass of sparkling cider and some Doritos to munch on."

"Doritos?" He laughs.

"Only the best here at Casa de Jimmy! They're Cool Ranch, buddy."

"Oh well, then..." He moves, somewhat reluctantly, into the living room. I follow and make sure he takes a seat on the couch. I hand him the remote. "You can watch something if you want. If our dinner isn't going to be a complete disaster, I need to work alone."

"I get it." He puts the remote beside himself on the couch. "Sure we can't have dessert first? Life is short and all that." He eyes me, a little grin turning up only one corner of his lips. It's sexy as hell, and I'm tempted, but no. Tonight is about swapping a night from hell with a night from heaven.

Miriam told me that heaven and hell are right here on earth, right now. And we always, always have the choice of which one we'll live in.

"We'll have plenty of dessert later. I promise."

I run back into the kitchen. I pour a glass of cider and return to Marc with it. I hand him the glass and set down the bowl of Doritos I have in my other hand. "Don't eat too many."

He smiles at me, and I can read the gratitude on his face. It warms me. Yet there's a part of me that still wonders, when he eyes me, when the other shoe's gonna drop and he'll know me and remember...

"Thanks." He takes a chip and eats it. Looks at me and cocks his head.

"What?" I ask.

He shrugs. "I don't know. It just struck me that you look familiar."

It doesn't matter that the words come out innocently enough; my stomach begins to churn. I give him what I know is a sick little grin. "I just have one of those faces."

Still queasy, I hurry back to the kitchen to get started on my salad.

Chapter Eight

MARC

One of those faces? One of those faces, he tells me? It didn't hit me until just that moment that there's something vaguely familiar about Jimmy. Maybe it was a movement he made, a gesture or the tilt of his head, but I had that unsettling feeling we label déjà vu.

Could I have met him before? Seen him somewhere? I scan my memories, at least the ones from when I lived here in Seattle. Could he be one of the many tricks I hooked up with when I was "playing the field" or, to be blunter, acting like a total slut?

There were a lot of guys back then. Too many. It's a wonder I stayed HIV negative, because I certainly wasn't always safe.

But even as I flip through the pages of my mental catalog of partners, Jimmy doesn't rise to the top. No bell rings. I shrug. Put the thought away. Maybe it's true—he simply reminds me of someone else.

But who?

Forget about it.

Jimmy pokes his head from out of the kitchen. "Supper's almost ready. You need a refill?"

I hold up my full glass. "I'm good. It smells delicious."

He waves away my compliment. "Ah. It's nothing. You want to eat in the kitchen or in here on the couch?"

He eyes the TV, and I pick up on the fact that he probably eats most of his meals in here, in front of the television. I surmise this because I do the same thing. It's what a lot of people who live alone do. The voices and the movement of the television, as pathetic a fact as it is, are company.

But we don't need that tonight. The kitchen has only a small table with two chairs, what my mom would call a "bistro set." They're made from molded plastic and obviously intended for an outdoor space, but their bright yellow color lends some cheer to the drab and desperately-in-need-of-an-update kitchen.

But the real cheer in that kitchen is Jimmy. I get up to join him. "Let's eat in the kitchen. I want to look at your pretty face across the table."

He snickers, and a rosy glow rises to his cheeks. I think I could love him.

*

We're about halfway through dinner when Jimmy says, "I shared a little bit about my growing up with you. Time to turn the tables, bud. I want to know more about you." He raises his glass to me and sits back a little, looking expectant.

"Dinner was excellent. That fish? Practically melted in my mouth. What did you do to it?"

"Just sautéed it with some salt and pepper, a little butter. It helps when you start out with good, fresh fish. It does all the work, just as long as you don't overcook it."

"And how do you avoid that?"

"The cook at the diner showed me how to test fish with my finger." He gets up and gently pokes my nose. "If it feels like the tip of your nose—that same hardness with just a little give—it's done. You can also look at it, and when it's just opaque, you know it's ready. Take it off the heat a little before that point and you're golden, because it'll continue cooking a little bit after it rests."

"You should be a chef."

Jimmy sighs. "I'd have to go to culinary school for that. And I can't afford it. Not even close. I barely make ends meet as it is." He raises his eyebrows, and again I have that feeling of familiarity as I look at him.

It fades quickly as he smiles and asks, "Why are you avoiding my question?"

Heat rises to my face. *Busted.* "What question?" I ask, trying to look innocent. Even as I make the attempt, I know I've failed.

"Don't do that," Jimmy says gently.

I'm tempted to ask "Don't do what?" but know I'd be pushing it and getting irritating. I shrug, eat some of the salad, which is also very good. "I don't know. My past wasn't very happy, but at least it was—" I stop as I ponder the right word. I don't want to insult him. I don't want to try to compare my so-called normal middle class life with his single-parent, growing-up-in-a-trailer one. I don't want to sound snobbish.

"At least it was what?" he asks.

"Stable," I say, letting the cards fall where they may. It hits me that I feel a little guilty about my privilege. Although we were by no means wealthy, or even anywhere close to it, I had a very normal upbringing.

"I lied," I said. Jimmy puts down his fork.

"I don't know why I said that about an unhappy upbringing. It's not true. You just poured out to me all about your family and all the trials you went through, and I wanted to be sympathetic and not make you feel bad by coming back with my happy home."

"That's stupid!" he says. "Why would you think you having a happy childhood would make me feel bad? Hell, I'm glad somebody did. Tell me about it."

I lean forward and give him the quick rundown of my past. I talk for much longer than I thought I—the quiet guy—was capable of. I tell him about growing up in a three-bedroom bungalow in the predominantly Jewish Chicago suburb of Skokie. How my parents had Ozzie and Harriet lives, from what I could see. "Dad was a CPA and worked downtown for an insurance company. And Mom stayed at home until I was in high school. Then she went out and got a real estate license and tried to make a go of selling houses. But I don't think her heart was ever in it. She never made much, and after a few years, she quit. She went back to staying at home, sold Mary Kay for a while, and then finally gave up." I stop, feeling myself strangely sad and wanting so badly to change the subject. I see my mother at the kitchen table, an ever-present glass of red wine at her elbow, watching a little portable TV we had on the counter. It seemed she watched everything from game shows to old sitcoms to reality TV, but what I remember was the faraway look in her eyes, as though she wanted to be anywhere but where she was. Sometimes I would ask her what she was watching, and there were times when she was actually startled. "Oh, I don't know. Some crap."

I feel an overwhelming burst of love for her—and melancholy. And I wonder what she really wanted from her life, what she dreamed of.

I should call her when I get home.

"But for the most part..." I lie again. "We were happy—nice Christmases, summer vacations, Bahamas cruises, a road trip to the Grand Canyon, summers up at Lake Geneva at my uncle's place." I give Jimmy a brave smile. "Boring—but happy. So American dream." Why am I saying this? Is there an American dream? Does anyone get to actually live it?

Then I tell him my own little side trip in my quest to snatch up a piece of that dream for myself—the way society told me the American dream was *supposed* to be lived. "I was married once."

"To a man or a woman?" Jimmy asks.

I hold up a finger, stopping him. "Back when this was, you wouldn't have even thought to ask that. I was just out of college. Lisa and I were college sweethearts from sophomore year on. We were each other's firsts, if you can believe that. And it wasn't bad, like you'd think. I enjoyed things with her. And I think I really did love her."

"But then you had the big old homo thing in the back of your head?"

"Well, that might not be the most delicate way of putting it, but yeah. The more I tried to deny I was, the harder that big old homo insisted on coming out." I stare down at my plate for a moment and then look back up at Jimmy. "We lasted less than a year. I broke her heart. I still carry that shame and guilt around with me."

"You didn't know. You were just trying to do what everyone expected of you."

I nod. And what he says is true, but I still can see Lisa's face in my mind, and just seeing that image causes a stab of self-recrimination to rise up inside, like real physical pain, which, I suppose, it is. I know my own lack of self-acceptance really hurt her, and I wonder if I can ever rationalize my guilt for that. She was a good and trusting woman. She didn't deserve what she got. And what she got was me.

I don't want to talk about this anymore. So I get up, cross to the other side of the table, and then stop in front of Jimmy. He peers up.

"Get up," I say softly.

He grins. "Why?"

"It's time for dessert."

I take his hand and pull him toward where I hope his bedroom is.

There's no resistance.

*

I wake later in the dark. Rain patters against the window, and I look over at Jimmy, on his back, mouth open and snoring. It feels like we're the only people in the world. Here, with Jimmy, I feel safe and secure. The rain only intensifies the feeling.

We went at it for what seemed like hours, getting lost in the sensation of each other's lips, tongues. We did everything possible two men can do—and then did it again.

I was top; he was bottom. He was top; I was bottom.

We tasted each other's sweat, skin, and come.

There was one point I remember where it seemed like I went completely out of my head, and I was nothing more than a huge patch of nerve endings being stimulated. I was so happy in that mindless moment of *right here, right now* that I wanted it to continue forever.

Amid the groans and sighs, he whispered that he loved me, and I answered back in kind. Maybe it was too soon. I didn't—and don't—care. It felt so right.

When we finished, we lay in each other's arms, sweat-drenched, breathing hard, and feeling something beyond connection, beyond happiness.

Bliss?

He fell asleep first. That was just a few minutes ago. It was this beautiful letting go, and I loved the fact he was comfortable enough to do it with his head on my chest and my arms around him. I drifted myself for a few minutes, and when I awoke, we were where we are right now. Him on his back, me watching.

The moment is marred only by a sudden—and fierce—urge to pee. Jesus, how can some bodily functions be so intense and delirious, magical really, while others seem so pedestrian? I will ponder this in the bathroom.

I very carefully sit up, moving away from Jimmy, and then set my feet on the gritty hardwood floor.

I look over at him. The light filtering in through the blinds casts slats of pale orange on his face from the streetlight outside. He stirs a little and then turns over on his side. His snoring stops. I suppress a yearning to reach out and let my fingertips run across the stubbled planes of his face, to caress the dampness of his lips.

I doubt that he'd mind, but for God's sake, let the poor guy get some rest! He's young. Good for at least one more round before the dusky pewter light of dawn creeps in. I grin to myself, and even after all we've done tonight, I start to get hard again.

I stand, my erection jutting out before me, and think how I'll have to sit on the toilet for a while to allow this situation to resolve itself before I can fully empty my bladder.

I creep from the bedroom, casting a glance over my shoulder a couple of times, but Jimmy doesn't wake. Part of me is glad, the other disappointed.

The hallway is dark. I grope my way along the wall. Behind one closed door, there's the soft murmur of a TV, and I think how Jimmy's roommate must have come home at some point. Did he hear us? How could he not?

Oh well. Jimmy told me he was gay as well. Two gay roommates probably wouldn't be too shocked by the sounds of coupling coming from another room. I just like to think that his roommate rarely hears it from Jimmy's room, if ever. Jealous much? I know there's already a connection, a little possessiveness on my part, and I wonder if I care too much, too soon.

But you know what? It doesn't matter. Jimmy's a gift. Who can blame me if I like to indulge the fantasy that he only has eyes—and lips, and dick, and ass—for me?

In the bathroom I sit down, waiting for my erection to subside. As I do so, I look around the room. It's small, cramped. The tile floor, small black-and-white diagonals, is most likely original to the building, which I would guess was built maybe as far back as the 1920s. Two towels, one red and one white, hang haphazardly from the towel rack on the wall. There's a claw-foot tub with a metal rod shower enclosure, an old wooden medicine cabinet that's seen too many coats of paint, a pedestal sink with separate hot and cold spigots. There's rust in the sink. In one corner there's a pair of jeans, balled up, and on top of it, a Seattle Seahawks hoodie. I wonder which of the guys the clothes belong to. The wastebasket, white plastic, is nearly overflowing.

I finally go. As I stand up and then turn around to shake off, I notice a little bar mounted above the toilet with hooks on it. Various things hang from the hooks—a few rubber bands, a cock ring—this makes me laugh—and an assortment of cheap leather jewelry: a braided wristband, a crystal on a leather strap to be worn around the neck. This last I finger, staring at it. I feel a tingling as I touch it, as if it's a talisman, transmitting energy to me.

And then I feel a little sick.

I used to have one just like it. I can see it in my mind's eye, in a black wooden box I had on my dresser, lying next to a watch I lost, assorted receipts, phone numbers, a black-and-red thumb drive.

The tingling switches to nausea. I plop back down, hard, on the toilet. I shut my eyes, trying to blot out the memory that rises up.

A couple of years ago, I invited a guy over to my apartment off Adam4Adam. When he arrived, I knew he was high as a kite. And he confirmed this shortly after I let him inside my place when he brought out a little glass pipe with black residue on the bottom, white residue along the stem. "You party?" he asked me, wiggling the pipe in my face.

I can see him in my mind's eye, and a cold blast runs up and down my spine. Sitting on my bed, naked, emaciated, so skinny his ribs showed, poking out through sallow skin. Long, blond, but somehow dirty-looking dreads, stretching almost down to his waist. He's holding the pipe to his lips, twisting it this way and that to swirl the drug inside, which his butane lighter has turned to liquid. Watching in a kind of horrified fascination as he exhales a huge white cloud. He offers me the pipe again.

I shake my head.

And his face.

It's Jimmy's face. The hair, the body, the sense of decay are all different from the Jimmy sleeping in the other room, the one I just fucked *on our second occasion in bed together*, yet they're him. The face is his. It may have filled out some, but it's the same.

Why didn't I see it before? Was it because I didn't want to? Because he's changed so much?

He'd called himself JD back then. The sex between us took only about ten minutes—at least for me. But JD wouldn't leave. He stayed, watching porn on my desktop computer, stroking, smoking that damn pipe, and occasionally scrolling through his phone.

He got a lot of texts.

Can I be mistaken? I shake my head, my heart beating faster, my breath coming a little quicker.

No.

You know how you see someone who you think looks like a person you know, and you think it could be them? But there's something instinctive in you that tells you it's not. The reverse is true too; when you see someone you know, you see the whole package, and you know, with pretty much certainty, that they are who you think they are.

I've reached that conclusion.

It's him.

And I want to puke.

The logical part of my brain wants to argue, urges me to look for more proof. I stand and notice a small, cheap cabinet, white particleboard, opposite. I open the bottom and find stacks of frayed, grayish, yet neatly folded towels. There's an old *Entertainment Weekly* on top of the towels, its page curled by damp. The drawer above creaks when I slide it open, and I shudder. There's a lot of crap inside—a beard trimmer, scissors, a box of Band-Aids, a tube of Neosporin, a lighter, a coupon for Nyquil.

And there's an iPod. It's in a rubberized black sleeve.

It's just like the one I used to have.

I have to sit back down. I clutch the iPod in my hand, willing it not to be mine.

When JD came over a couple of years ago, he not only terrified me by refusing to leave, but he stole from me. Every chance he got. I wondered why he brought along the big black backpack when he showed up. I assumed it had sex toys in it, and later, his drug paraphernalia.

Turned out it was most likely empty so he could fill it with my stuff when I left the room.

He took a Fossil watch I loved, an emerald ring that had belonged to my grandfather, all the cash in my wallet. I knew the amount—$200—because I'd gone to the ATM that day after work. He took stupid stuff—running shorts, a souvenir T-shirt I'd gotten in Mexico, a leather rope with a crystal attached to it. He pocketed an expensive pair of Bluetooth headphones, Ray-Ban sunglasses, a couple of thumb drives with porn on them I'd left lying by the computer.

He took a whole lot of shit, none of which I'd discovered until he'd left, early in the morning, as I begged him to go.

Right now I feel the same sickness in the pit of my gut—violation. The food he'd made for me tonight churns around inside.

I look down at the iPod, exactly like the one I'd lost that night. I rub my finger along its rubberized cover, debating whether I really want to wake it up. Right now I could still bury my head in the sand—not really, but I still don't have concrete proof. But if I scroll through the playlists on this thing, it would be proof enough, verification enough, that the guy I just slept with, the one I thought I was falling in love with, was the same guy who'd left me feeling sick and violated two years ago. Not so much because he took my things—nothing was that valuable, and everything, save for my grandpa's ring, was replaceable. But because I invited him in, and he betrayed me and used me.

It took me months to get over the trauma. It replayed over and over again, on endless loop, in my head. I was celibate for three months afterward, fearful that I'd be violated again. I tried getting in touch with him to see if there was a way I could maybe at least get my grandpa's birthstone ring back, but he'd blocked me everywhere he could. Or he just had gotten what he'd wanted from me and had nothing more to say. We both knew he was a thief.

I sigh. There's no turning back now.

I press the silver button in the center of the iPod, and its little screen illuminates. There they are. My playlists:

> Hi-Energy
>
> Gym/Workout
>
> 80s
>
> Favorite Females Pop
>
> Favorite Females Jazz
>
> Classical mellow
>
> Big Band Jazz
>
> Trance/Electronica
>
> Dance Ass Off
>
> Run

All my playlists. This isn't a coincidence. I frown. This is my iPod. The weird thing? I feel numb. Back then, when I discovered JD had robbed me, I felt rage. I felt violated, betrayed. Sick. But maybe I got that all out at the time, because now, as I stare down at the iPod, scrolling through the old songs and artists I'd once painstakingly uploaded, creating multiple playlists to suit any mood, all I feel is—nothing.

And the need, pretty urgent, that I have to get out of here. The bathroom's walls closing in on me, like some kind of old horror movie. It's hard to breathe.

I don't flush. I clutch the iPod in my hand as I creep softly back to the bedroom. I wince as the door creaks when I open it, praying Jimmy doesn't wake. I don't know what I'd say to him. I don't know what I'd do.

Numb? Maybe not so much now as I stand here at the foot of his little twin bed, looking down on him. He's kicked the covers partially off, and one leg, hairy, well-formed, lies exposed.

"Who are you?" I whisper.

And I wonder if he even has any memory of me. Or if I was just one in a long line of drug-crazed tricks he abused and abandoned.

At some point in his life, he must have cleaned himself up. It's not only the fact that he won't even touch a drop of alcohol in my presence, it's the healthy vitality that seems to radiate off him now. I'm not surprised it took me a while to recognize him, although I think there was something nagging at me from the first moment I saw him in the diner that morning, a sense that I knew him from somewhere. It was like when you watch TV and see a guest star who looks familiar but you have no clue from where.

Good for you, I send out to him telepathically. *Good for you for cleaning yourself up. But I can't forget what you did to me. And I certainly can't forgive.*

I gather my clothes up from the floor, making sure I have everything. I creep back to the living room, where I dress quickly, praying the roommate or Jimmy won't decide to get up for a bathroom break or midnight snack run.

Thunder rumbles outside. It mirrors the turmoil in my gut, my heart.

I pat my pockets, making sure my keys and my wallet are where they should be.

I am about to start out the door when I remember the iPod. I'd put it on an end table while I got dressed but then picked it up again. I clutch it. I look down at it and contemplate taking it home. It is, after all, indisputably mine.

But no. I think the little device will serve as good as anything else as a farewell note, a not-so-obscure "fuck you." I tiptoe back to Jimmy's room, glad I left the door partially open. I move close to the bed, where a pile of books serves as a nightstand, and set the iPod down in the center of the top one.

Just as I'm leaving, I hear the bedclothes rustle. I turn to see Jimmy lifting his head from the pillow, and my heart clutches. The amazing thing? A part of me wants desperately to get back into bed with him, to discover that somehow, some way, I was mistaken. That he will fill my gullible heart with lies I want so desperately to believe that I will.

"Hey," he says, his voice deep, raspy with sleep and exhaustion.

"Hey," I say back, trying not to display the tension thrumming in me as though it's electric. I put one hand on the door. I taste a splash of bile at the back of my throat.

"Where you goin'?" he asks.

"Bathroom," I tell him.

He lies back down and turns over on his side. "Hurry back."

"I will. I will, Jimmy."

I hurry to close the door, afraid it will reach his sleep-addled brain that I'm fully clothed. I don't look back. I head straight for the front door and out—into the night. Into a world where I wonder if I'll ever feel safe to care for another man again.

This shit isn't worth it, I think as I step onto the sidewalk, and the rain, pouring down, soaks me instantly.

I don't care.

Even though my apartment is at least three miles from here, I decide to walk home.

Chapter Nine

JIMMY

The first thought that hits me, even before I open my eyes, is *Shit. I have to get to work.*

The second one, scarier, is *I'm alone in bed.*

I turn and open my eyes to bright sunlight. The room is awash in it. Dust motes practically sparkle in the air. The sun shimmers around the edges of the blinds and makes me think of summer. There's a rising sense of anticipation in me, until…

I look over at the empty space in bed beside me and frown. I run my hand over the pillow and the sheet.

They're cold.

He's in the bathroom. He's got to be in the bathroom. He wouldn't just creep out like some one-night stand. That's not Marc. That's not my Marc. He wouldn't just leave without saying goodbye.

Would he?

I lie back, breathe in. I wish I didn't crave a smoke, but I do. I sit up and rub my eyes, listening. The apartment is still. Outside, early morning traffic whizzes by on Western Avenue. Distant, a siren blares. I can hear a garbage truck's machinery working to whisk away another week of dumpster refuse.

The sun's brightness informs me I've overslept and missed starting time at the diner. I'm already making excuses—my alarm didn't go off—as I put my feet on the floor and bend over to grab my jeans, still balled up at the side of the bed.

I snort a quick burst of laughter. No wonder I overslept. I was *overserved* last night. Overserved with sex. Jesus! I was exhausted. *Am* exhausted. I can't remember the last time I was this wrung out—and I'm happy about it.

I grope around in my jeans pockets until I find my lighter and a pack of Marlboro Blacks. I stand and pull the jeans on and head for the front door, thinking I'll see or hear Marc in the bathroom as I pass by. I picture myself rapping a couple of times on the door and asking what he wants for breakfast. I'd thought ahead—ever-hopeful—yesterday when I ran to the store and got some eggs, orange juice, bacon, and instant coffee.

But when I get to the bathroom, the door's open. The emptiness of the little room mocks me. I peek inside anyway, not quite understanding why. I mean, it's not like Marc's going to be hiding behind the shower curtain. I pull the shower curtain anyway, and all I see is a leaking faucet and a bar of soap that's little more than a sliver.

Kevin's door is closed, but I hear him snoring. His TV, never off, creates a low hum beneath the sound of him sawing logs.

I step out the apartment front door, hurry through the vestibule and then outside. The air smells clean, brisk, washed after last night's rain.

I sit on the top step and light up, watch the gray cloud of smoke as it emerges from my mouth and my nostrils, how the wind snatches it away. The streets are still slick from last night's downpour.

I tell myself one of two things to try to explain why Marc wasn't next to me in bed. First, he had the presence of mind to wake up and get himself off to work. One of us has to be responsible! Somewhere in that little cubbyhole I call a bedroom, he left me a note. Of course he did. Or a text... And I curse myself for not bringing my phone outside.

I barely smoke half the cigarette before I stand and pitch it down to the sidewalk. I'm too keyed up to finish it. Now, littering's something I normally wouldn't do. Usually I'd put my smoke out on the wall or the step below me and carry it back in to dispose of responsibly in the trash.

But I'm anxious, nerves jittering like a horde of bees unloosed in my brain. My second thought—that Marc was in the kitchen as I passed through the apartment, searching for coffee or some other form of sustenance— needs to be desperately proven right.

Right now.

Heart pounding, I take a deep breath and step back in, knowing even as I hurry for no good reason that he won't be there.

Something happened. He knows. The two thoughts are so simple, yet so terrifying.

The kitchen's empty. Plates from last night's dinner fill up the sink, rinsed and waiting to be washed. I left the salad dressing out on the counter overnight, and I put it back in the fridge. I look around myself again, absurdly thinking *he's hiding somewhere*, ready to jump out and startle me, laughing.

How I wish that could be true!

I hug myself, shivering, even though it's not really cold in the apartment, running my hands up and down my arms. Dread, like some little creature digging its tiny razor-sharp claws into my brain, begins to make a nest.

I return to the bedroom, ready to snatch up my phone. Surely a text will be waiting for me. *Hey...last night was amazing. But I had to run out so I could make it into work on time. You were sleeping so soundly I didn't want to wake you.* An emoji of a face blowing a heart-shaped kiss. *See you soon!*

I look around for my phone and spy it on the floor. Good thing I didn't step on it. I pick it up and press the Home button, but no message is waiting. Just to be sure, I key in my pass code and go to the messages app. Nothing. And there are no missed calls either.

What the fuck?

I sit on my bed, dejected. It's then I see the iPod, lying there like a snake coiled and waiting to strike.

I swear to God, my heart drops from its place in my chest to somewhere down around my groin. Bile rises up, acidic, bitter, burning, and I taste a little of the fish we had last night. It makes me want to puke.

I stare at the iPod for a long time, not touching it, as though I feel it's electrified and the simple act of touching it will send a charge straight to my heart.

I know what it means. Everything rushes back. That night with him two years ago. I fenced most everything I took from him—that was my modus operandi. But I kept three things—a pair of Under Armour gym shorts, gray and lime green, a crystal on a leather strap, and the iPod. For a while I listened to his playlists at all hours, dancing around the bathroom as I got ready for yet another hookup.

And then I got clean.

I didn't have some hitting-bottom moment like some folks do. I simply woke up one day feeling depleted, like it was hard to breathe, and knew I needed to get help. I'd seen enough addiction growing up to know that particular demon had managed to possess me, too, despite my personal history.

I went to my first Narcotics Anonymous meeting that day—in the basement of a church not far from where I now work. Scared and trembling, I forced myself to go in. I didn't speak to a soul and sat in the back the whole time, hoping for invisibility.

People talk about relapse, but I never did. Someone in the group said something that very first meeting that I always remember, that I always cling to— *You'll get sober when you want* not *to use more than you want to use.*

The days, the weeks, the months *not* using started to accumulate.

The iPod ended up in a drawer in the bathroom. I'd always intended to get rid of it, because it, more than anything else, was a reminder of Marc.

Maybe I should take that back about never hitting bottom. Maybe hitting bottom, for me, was the moment I left his apartment, my backpack weighed down with his shit. Not because I fucked him and stole from him, but because I cared about him. See, he was the first guy I hooked up with during that time who I really cared about. The other losers? They were always in it for the drugs they could get off me, and I rationalized my stealing from them as payment for product.

I hooked up again after him. I used again—many times after him. I ripped off gullible dudes—mostly older—time and time again.

But I never forgot Marc.

Never forgot that night, lying next to him in bed while he slept, my own heart hammering in my chest from the drug. I lay there and watched him and thought *What a beautiful man.*

I hated his cleanliness. Hated his innocence. Hated his normal life.

But in spite of the hatred, I wanted his life. And I realized—very gradually and not just then and there—that such a life was out of reach for me. As long as I was enslaved to that stupid, corrosive drug, that combination of drain cleaner and antifreeze that made me into someone else, I would never be able to have a normal life again.

I would either go on and die, or I would quit.

I chose to quit.

I pick up the iPod, run my hand over its rubber surface and bring it to life. The battery, surprisingly, still has some juice, but it's almost dead. There's enough time for me to look at his playlists again and for me to recall listening to his music. The songs always reminded me of him, of that night when I was unable to make myself leave his side, even though staying put was putting me in danger of getting caught.

I wanted him. I wanted his life.

I set the iPod back down and feel the tears running down my face. I hadn't even noticed them before. *I am a piece of shit. I deserve this.* And maybe that's why I never got rid of the iPod—to ensure I got punished. Maybe there was a piece of me inside that remembered it was in that drawer in the bathroom, just waiting for him to find when he was over.

I lie on the bed and allow myself to wallow in self-pity, sobbing. I curl into a fetal position and just let it all out, knowing a guy like Marc could never want a turd like me. And here's the proof.

He's gone. And what can I possibly say to him?

After a while I sit up, lean against the wall beside my bed, and call work, report off, saying I'm not feeling well, which has to be the understatement of the century.

And then I call Miriam.

As soon as she answers, with her cheery "Hey babe! What's up?" I start crying again, choking out the words, telling her what happened. She listens, as she always does, and I can hear her sympathy, her lack of judgment, her warmth, coming through the phone all the way from the east side.

The door creaks open, and I look up to see Kevin standing there. He's wearing a T-shirt with a yellow stain on the belly and an old pair of faded red plaid boxers. His eyebrows are together in concern.

I continue to babble to Miriam, saying shit like "I've lost him" and "It's just what I deserve" over and over again.

Kevin sits on the foot of my bed. He reaches out a tentative hand, like you'd do if you were approaching a wild animal. His hand hovers a bit above and finally lands on my calf. He strokes it, the sympathy in his face only making me cry harder.

"Who are you talking to?" he asks, voice soft, filled with concern.

"Miriam. You know, my sponsor."

He scoots closer and pries the phone from my hand. He glances briefly at the screen and tosses it on the bed.

I sit up straighter and wipe some of the snot off my face with the back of my hand. "What are you doing?"

"*I'm* your sponsor, Jimmy." He stares at me, waiting for it to sink in.

I close my eyes, the grief rising up in my chest like a physical thing. I flop back on the bed and turn to face the wall. "I know. Don't you think I know that?"

He puts his hand on my shoulder and squeezes. "Miriam—" he begins.

And I finish for him, just to prove to him that I'm not *that* crazy. "Miriam's dead. She died in a car crash on the Aurora Bridge a year ago. Too much Oxy and vodka. Went out in a blaze of glory."

He squeezes my shoulder again. The sheets rustle as he lies behind me and wraps his arms around me, pulling my back close to his chest.

We lie like that, spooning, for a long time. And I remember Miriam, her dyed red hair, her sweet smile, and how she couldn't beat her demons. They finally took her.

"I know she's gone," I whisper into the pillow. "I'm not that fucked up. But I still like to talk to her." I turn to Kevin and give him a little smile. "She listens. And, weirdly enough, she always knows just what to say."

"Oh, sweetie," Kevin says, reaching over to brush some of the tears off my face. "I'm here for you. And I may not always know just what to say, but I listen. And I try my best."

"I know you do."

"What happened?" he asks.

I sit up and hand him the iPod. "This happened."

He looks down at the little square in his hand, confused. "I don't get it."

I tell him everything—all about how I came into possession of it two years ago. Everything. I don't paint myself in a good light. How could I?

He puts the iPod back on the stack of books. "He found it?"

"Yeah, I was too stupid to get rid of it." I snort out a bitter laugh. "How could I fence it? What would an old iPod bring anyway? A quarter? Nobody uses those things anymore."

"Did he say anything? Accuse you?"

"He left it lying right there where you just put it. And then he got the hell out and away from me. I don't blame him!" I smile. "He's a smart guy. Leaving it there was all he needed to say."

Kevin sits up and then stands. "I'm sorry, man. I know you liked him."

"Liked him? I think I was falling in love."

Kevin nods. "So what are you gonna do?"

"What can I do?"

"You could get in touch with him. Apologize. Tell him you were a different person then."

"Make amends to someone I've harmed?" I ask, echoing one of the twelve steps so familiar to us both.

He laughs. "Something like that."

"I don't know, Kev. Him slipping out and leaving that for me to find sends a pretty straightforward message, and that message isn't *I can't wait to see you again.* Right?"

Kevin nods. He sits back on the bed. "You want my advice?"

I turn away from him again to face the wall, sighing. "I don't know."

"Sure you do." He places a hand on my shoulder and pushes down, forcing me to roll over and meet his gaze. "First, don't use this as a trigger. This would be a great time to tell yourself you could use a little oblivion and—"

I put a hand up to cut him off. "Ain't gonna happen. Two years, Kev, two years, I'm not gonna throw that away."

"Well, just be mindful. That little addict in your brain is still there, always will be. And he's probably already plotting how to use this to his advantage."

"You sound like Miriam."

He cocks his head.

"If she were alive, of course. But I remember her saying similar things."

"Just let me know, buddy, if you want to go to a meeting. No, make that *when* you want to go to a meeting, which today sounds like a real good idea." He gives me an expectant look.

"I don't know, Kev. Let me think about it."

"I don't want to leave you alone."

"I'll be fine!" I snap. "Fuck." And then: "I'm sorry. I don't mean to blow up at you."

He says gently, "You're *not* fine. You talk to dead people, for Christ's sakes. This thing, whatever it is, shook you up."

I snort. "That's putting it mildly." And then I launch into self-pity mode. I know it even as the words begin to tumble from my lips, but I can't help myself. "It's just that the last two years—two fuckin' years—have been about one thing—recovery. Well, work and recovery. Waiting tables, cleaning up after other people's shit, going to meetings, day in and day out. And then I finally meet someone who brings a little joy into my life—real joy, you know what I mean, man? Not the kind of artificial high at the end of a meth pipe, but the chance for *real* happiness, and what happens? I reach out for it, barely thinking I deserve it. And fate slaps my hand away."

"Oh, poor you. What? You think falling in love's going to solve all your troubles?"

"Says the perpetually single guy..."

"Shut up. I don't have to tell you, and *Miriam* would say the same thing, that your happiness has to come from inside. Not from a pipe. Not from a guy." He pokes my chest. "But from *in here*. Your heart."

"Ah, I don't need the NA shit. *My* heart is breaking!" I shout.

"Yeah, mister, you do need the NA shit, maybe now more than ever. Now, when the ghosts of your fucked-up past have arrived to haunt you, when the damage you did is finally coming home to roost."

He exits the room suddenly and dramatically. *What the fuck?* I wonder.

He comes back after a few minutes, long enough for me to wonder if he's coming back at all.

"I just checked online. There's a meeting over in Fremont, at the Baptist church, in an hour. Get up, get showered, and get ready. We'll Uber. My treat."

I stare down at my sheets—at the dark stains left by last night—and my heart seizes up again. "Sure. You're right," I say. "You go ahead and shower first." As I say the words, I think of all the times in meetings I heard addiction described as cunning, baffling, and powerful. And even as I think it, I'm plotting.

I only hope Kevin doesn't catch on. Miriam would have.

I lie on my back, waiting to hear the bathroom door close and the hiss of the shower. When I know Kevin is under water and safely out of the way, I get dressed in a pair of jeans, a T-shirt, and my Cons. I check that my phone's battery has enough juice.

At the front door, I grab my denim jacket off the hook. I drop my phone in its inner pocket and start to head outside.

Then I remember and head back in. I grab the phone's charger—I may be gone for a while—and my smokes.

Outside, the sunlight has given up the ghost. The blue skies and sunshine the day began with are gone. Now heavy lead-colored clouds press in, threatening rain.

I stick my hands in my pockets and start down toward the waterfront, sick with fear of my own damn self.

Thursday

Chapter Ten

MARC

I wake to sunshine. Brilliant. Summerlike. *Let's celebrate!*

Appropriate? Hell no.

Today's the kind of day that *should* be what one would order up for a funeral—gray, low-hanging clouds, lots of rain, everyone walking at a dazed, zombified pace, carrying big black umbrellas, garbed in all black as well. There should be a cold wind out of the north, blowing trash and rusty tin cans along the street. If I turned on the radio, the music that would play would be dirgelike or one of Leonard Cohen's more downbeat songs. Or perhaps, since I'm gay, a Sondheim selection. "Send in the Clowns"?

Ah, fuck it.

I'm lying in bed, half staring out my window, half dozing in a depressed, disappointed, down state. I came home, drenched, just a few hours ago. Heedless of my soaked state, I collapsed into bed. Despite the trauma of my discovery about Jimmy, I fell quickly into a deep sleep. I have vague memories of dreams, and all I can recall from them is the terror of outstretched hands, trying to grab me.

Now, outside, the sun glints off Lake Union, causing sparkles to shimmer on the water's surface, as though someone cast diamonds upon it. I rented this place because every window looked out on the inner city's big lake. I've always considered myself fortunate to have found my place, even though it's a small one bedroom with about 850 square feet. Yet the view is killer—boats on the water, seaplanes landing and taking off, rowing crews out in the early morning. Sunrises that can be a riot of orange, deep blue, violet, and slate gray. Rainbows across the water. Gas Works Park, a little south.

Now I just resent the view. It's so pretty—with this sunlight that's so especially wrong for winter, for Christ's sake—and it mocks me.

I know I should be getting up, hitting the shower, making a smoothie, and heading out to Dexter Avenue to catch the #62 bus downtown. My normal routine. But today's not normal. We are having our very own real-life Throwback Thursday here—and the picture is not pretty.

I feel like I can't move. Lethargy has a death grip on my limbs. I could lie in this bed all day, and I'm really, really tempted to do just that. A smoothie? God, I'm not even hungry enough to down something that's mostly liquid, even if I made it a sweet one with bananas, peanut butter, almond milk, and a little stevia for good measure. And a shower? Who cares how clean I am? I may never shower again.

I turn over in bed, away from the view, and give out a forlorn laugh at myself and my misery.

He's just another guy. Don't beat yourself up about it. I know you're disappointed and you thought there was some there there. But there isn't...and there wasn't. He's a loser, a creep, a drug addict. Except for the last thing, he's like most of the guys you have the bad luck to meet, which is why you've been kind of off the market for the last several months.

I turn back over and stare at the blue sky, the striated clouds drifting slowly by, trying to force my mind to go blank. I read a book last fall, *The Four Agreements*, which was about four agreements you make with yourself that are supposed to transform your life into something better, something worthwhile, a life worth living, free of pain.

The one agreement I'm trying to get to sink in at the moment, as I stare out at the sky is—*don't take anything personally*.

That's a difficult one right now. How can I not take Jimmy—or JD, as he called himself two years ago when he ripped me off and left me feeling violated and betrayed—personally? How can I *not* look at our renewed acquaintance as yet another betrayal, this one even more cutting because I know he had to have realized who I was right from the start. Was it all a setup? Is he back in his pathetic little apartment right now with his mysterious "roommate," laughing it up while sharing a bowl and watching porn?

I close my eyes and tell myself to breathe. Just breathe. I'm getting myself so worked up about all of this. Can you blame me? Yet, yet...I try to tell myself that *The Four Agreements* made sense to me when I first read it.

And yes, if I just breathe and allow myself to think, I can reasonably say that taking Jimmy's deceit and thievery personally is a waste of time. Because it's *not* personal. The dude is fucked up. He's got issues, and that's putting it mildly. Drugs are probably the least of his problems. He told me a little bit about his background...

Believe it or not, compassion wells up in me as I think of him as a little boy in a run-down trailer with an alcoholic mom. It sounds like something out of a *Lifetime* movie. And maybe it was, I think, shaking my head. Maybe it was.

How do I know anything he said was true?

I want to let it go. Let *him* go. Erase meeting him *again*. But just like two years ago, when he stole every little thing he could get his hands on, I know I won't be able to simply chalk it up to experience and move on, because that's not me.

You hurt me, and I feel the sting.

There are bruises, even if they're just metaphorical.

I sit up, feet on the floor. I left the window open last night, and a breeze sneaks in through the screen. At least it's cold, causing goose bumps to rise on my arms.

My stomach churns again.

My heartbeat feels irregular.

I'm taking things personally.

The cold wind has brought with it a bank of gray clouds, moving in slowly to obliterate the blue sky and sunshine. Now that's more like it.

The answer to all of this, I believe, is to get moving. Do something. Lying in bed brooding and feeling sorry for myself isn't going to improve anything. I have to accept this loss, and I will eventually, but just like the incident with him two years ago, it will take time. I can't kid myself into thinking I can simply shrug my shoulders and tell myself he's an asshole and resume my regularly scheduled programming.

No.

I will need time to process. To feel, really feel, my pain.

And right now I need to get to work. Get up. One foot in front of the other. Bathroom first. Shower, shave, make that sad mug you call a face presentable to the world. Eat something. Dress. Head out. Catch the bus.

Look at me. I have a plan.

*

"So the best way to get *over* a man is to get under one." Don smears pimento cheddar spread on the large pretzel he ordered as an appetizer. He stares at me, a grin playing about his lips and expectation in his eyes. He's waiting for me to nod and indicate I agree with his sage, canned, Blanche Devereaux advice.

"Oh, come on." I'm not in the mood. I pick at my Caesar salad, bringing a parmesan crouton to my mouth. Normally savory and delicious, today the crouton tastes like nothing—deep-fried cardboard, maybe.

We're having lunch—Don's treat—at Brave Horse Tavern in South Lake Union. When I rolled into the office twenty minutes late, Don noticed my demeanor immediately. Before I even sat down, his head popped up over our shared cubicle and he asked, "Who died?"

Sometimes I think Don doesn't have an original thought in his head. Thank God his heart is in the right place, though. We went for coffee, and I spilled the whole sordid story as we sat outside Starbucks at one of the three small metal table and chair sets out there.

He listened without being a smartass. He wasn't even judgmental about my letting JD into my house once upon a time, other than musing that a "pretty face can open many doors." Fact was, he could have called me stupid, naïve, overly trusting. He could have said I had been thinking, as usual, with my dick instead of my head—the big one, up top. He could have chastised me for being too trusting, told me I got off easy, and that it was lucky I lived to tell the tale. He could have very reasonably asked what the fuck was wrong with me.

He would have been right to ask every one of those questions.

But he didn't. He only placed a chubby, pinky-ring hand over mine and cocked his head—his way of showing sympathy.

"I've never shared this with anyone before," I told him in a weak little voice barely above a whisper. "I was always so ashamed about what happened. I just wanted to forget."

"You have nothing to be ashamed of, honey. You didn't do anything wrong." He grins for a moment. "Other than looking for love in all the wrong places." He took another bite, chewed, and then said, "We *all* do that."

Now he goes on to inform me of the same stuff I told myself this morning, through a mouthful of fried chicken sandwich. The advice and the image of his half-eaten food are both rather ugly and unsettling. Even if the advice is true.

"No, seriously. Go out on a date. Get laid. Let yourself go. Be a wanton slut. Be one for me." His expression goes a little wistful, his gaze faraway. "Please." And I wonder if he's thinking he wishes he had my problems.

"I don't know." The course of action he's proposing has about as much appeal as this salad before me. It all but turns my stomach. I bring up the four agreements because I'd read the book at his urging.

I force myself to take a bite of salad, chew, and swallow. I can eat if I make it mechanical like this. "I'm trying not to take it personally."

"You shouldn't." He gets out his phone and scrolls. "Ah," he says. "Here it is. My own little Throwback Thursday." He sets the phone on the table. I look down to see a picture of a much-younger Don. I only recognize the man because he's showed me pictures from his San Francisco past before.

"Wasn't he gorgeous?" Don taps the picture on his screen. "Time's a bitch!" He bursts into laughter.

The man in the picture bears no resemblance to the man sitting across from me now. Young Don is blindingly handsome, with thick blond hair, a porn-star handlebar mustache, a tan to die for—I'm not kidding—and perfect white teeth. It's obvious he's at least forty pounds lighter, even though it's a head shot. He's wearing a blue shirt of some satiny fabric, unbuttoned halfway down so you can see his smooth-muscled chest. A thick gold chain encircles his neck.

"You were hot," I say, agreeing out loud only with the first of his assertions, even though I have to sadly agree with the second as well.

"*Were* being the operative word. Don't apologize. No one knows the truth better than yours truly.

"That was somewhere around the late seventies, early eighties. You wouldn't know it by looking at me, but I was the biggest cokehead in the Castro. I had a dealer—gorgeous Turkish man—who would show up in his BMW outside my apartment and deliver an eight ball anytime of the day or night. He was outside my place so often, people in my building were beginning to think he was my boyfriend, even if he was as straight as they come." Don sighs. "Believe me, I know. I tried to seduce him more than once."

"Why are you telling me this?"

He shrugs. "Because I'm a big old drug addict myself, sweetie." He hastens to add, "Recovering, of course. We're always recovering." He finishes up his sandwich and casts a gaze across the table at my salad like it's prey. "You gonna finish that?"

I slide it across to him. He continues eating and talking. "I'm telling you this because you really shouldn't take what this JD or Jimmy fella did personally because, honey, his behavior is all about him, not you."

"It would be pretty to think so," I say.

"No. No. I am serious. I know what it's like—addiction. And I can tell you two things.

"One, nobody asks to be an addict. Just like nobody asks for cancer.

"And two, when we're high, we are *not* ourselves. Drugs, especially shit like meth and coke, take over. They possess you just like that demon in *The Exorcist*. Yeah...they turn normally nice people into monsters." For once Don's composure falters, and I can see the scared confusion and sadness in his expression, even if he tries to quickly divert my attention by staring down at the table and taking another bite of salad.

When he looks up to return his gaze to me, his eyes are glassy with tears. "Let me tell you what I did."

"You don't have to."

"No. I think you should know. So you understand exactly why you mustn't take this personally.

"I almost died," he says, his usually loud voice pitched just above a whisper. His gaze shifts to the big window in front of us that looks out on Terry Avenue, where a streetcar passes by. Some people call it the SLUT, short for Seattle Lake Union Trolley, even though it's not properly a trolley. But the acronym is oddly appropriate for our conversation.

"You did? When was this?" I seldom touch my friend, and I realize that's a failing in me. Because he's older, I often let him take the mentor/parent/comforter role, and I realize, guiltily, that I'm seldom there for him in the same way. I squeeze his hand.

"Back in the eighties, hon, when we were all doin' coke like there was no tomorrow. And for me, there almost wasn't!" He chortles, but the mirth doesn't reach his eyes, which look sad in contrast.

"Anyway, it's an old story. Weekend-long binge at my place. I snorted up an eight ball while plying my trade on the phone sex line." He laughs again. "You probably don't even know about those! Not with Grindr and Scruff and Craigslist around these days. But back then, we pioneers who wanted a quick hookup and to have our dick delivered like a pizza, we called the 900 numbers." He shrugged. "It worked surprisingly well, much the same as being online does now. Minus the pictures, of course."

"Anyway, I had this one guy over, and he brought his own stash. I was in heaven. He was a hot Italian with a nine-inch dick, and I felt like it was snowing cocaine. We were drinking tequila and beer and trying to get our dicks hard. It was stupid. No Viagra back then either, and coke isn't exactly good for getting or keeping an erection. Still... We kept snorting, line after line, chasing that dragon, knowing that when at least one of our dicks got hard, bliss awaited us both.

"Except after this one big line, I suddenly felt like I couldn't breathe. I fell onto the floor, clutching my chest. No matter how hard I tried, I just couldn't draw any air into my lungs." I can see the panic in his eyes as he remembers.

"Good thing you weren't alone."

"Oh, but I was. I was! My big-dicked friend saw my condition, got worried, and took a powder, no pun intended."

"He just left you laying there?" I asked, disbelieving. "You could have died."

"Tell me about it. I probably would have, too, if my buddy hadn't had at least a little remorse and called—anonymously, of course—from a phone booth at the corner." He laughs. "A phone booth! Yet another blast from the past! Anyway, he did do me the kindness of calling an ambulance. And even if he was a coward and didn't stick around to see if I was okay or, God forbid, try to help me, he *did* save my life."

Don goes quiet for a while, and I can see how vivid the memory is for him, even all these years later. He shakes his head. "He saved my life in more ways than one. I mean, physically, I had started into cardiac arrest, but the way he really saved me was by helping me hit bottom. The docs said if my buddy hadn't made that call when he did, I'd have died right there on my living room floor."

"I'm so sorry, Don."

"Don't be. I got clean after that. Thank God!"

We sit in silence for a few minutes. I know it's time to head back to work, regardless of the revelations that have gone down between us.

"You know why I told you this story?"

"Probably. But why don't you tell me?"

He throws down three twenties on the table. "C'mon, we're gonna be late. I'll tell you on the way back."

It's a fairly long walk, and along the way, Don reiterates that he was so into his drugs back then, he almost killed himself for them. "And what happened wasn't totally accidental. I mean, especially that night, I knew I was crossing a line, doing way more than I should. Hell, I had tissue stuffed up my nose at one point because of the blood! And even with that, I kept doing it, willing to risk my life to chase after that high. So stupid!"

I nod.

"But you know what? You know what this has to do with your friend? And not taking things personally?"

I finish for him. "He was out of his head."

Don squeezes my shoulder as we walk. "Right." He stops and turns me to him. "From what you told me, he's not the person he was two years ago. You need to remember that."

I don't say anything until we get back to work, until we're in our cubicles. Until right now, as I stand and look over my cubicle and say softly to Don, "Thanks for today. And I know you're right. I just don't know that I can forgive and forget. Something's broken, and I'm not sure it can be fixed."

He nods. But then he just turns back to his computer. I guess his silence is saying a lot—the biggest thing is that I need to figure things out for myself, decide what's right for me.

*

It doesn't come to me until I'm lying in bed that night.

I don't know if I'm an addict, but I did have my problems, with sex, with porn, with love...with wanting all three so badly, and sometimes simultaneously, that I made unhealthy choices. I threw common sense out the window in pursuit of them. I chased after them when I was pretty sure I didn't even want them.

I'm not sure why I did the last, but lying here now, with no one to contradict me, to tell me what a good guy I am, I can see I had my own addictive tendencies.

So maybe I wasn't much better than JD that night.

We'd met on Adam4Adam.

I remember how I was back then. I just couldn't seem to keep off the site. As soon as I got home from work, I logged on, and often I'd be on far into the night, sometimes forgoing dinner, dragging myself to bed in the wee hours of the morning, eyes red from staring at the monitor. The only thing that might have saved me from that fate was if, in fact, I had quote-unquote normal plans like going out to dinner or a movie with a friend like Don, or if scrolling through all those dick and ass pictures netted me a hookup.

Hookups happened a lot, too, back in those days. There was an endless parade of guys in and out of my bedroom, some nice, some not so nice, some out of my league, and some so far beneath me I'd be embarrassed if anyone in my building saw me letting them in.

It seems pretty much all my free time back in those days was wrapped up in chasing dick online.

And the night Jimmy—or JD—came over was no different.

I'd noticed his profile before. But I was always a little intimidated by it. I mean, he was pretty rough looking, with his piercings and his dreadlocks. There were not only those things, but his pictures were all of him in kind of rough-trade getups—leather chaps, combat boots, mirrored aviator sunglasses, with a leatherman biker cap pulled low over his eyes.

He was a little scary.

And I remember that night feeling like he was not only what I needed, but what I deserved. That deserved part? That's just coming to me now in retrospect.

I crossed a line that night. I wanted someone hard-edged, maybe a little mean. I wanted a man who was outside my comfort zone of white-bread normalcy.

And so, instead of responding to the perfectly nice guy in Green Lake whose profile pic was not of his dick, but of him on Alki Beach in West Seattle, skipping a stone across the Sound, I shot a message to JD.

And set things in motion.

I don't think we exchanged more than a few messages before he had my address and was headed over. I remember him asking me if I partied, and I was so naïve at the time that I thought he meant drinking or maybe smoking a little weed.

You'd think, from cruising sex lines and hookup sites, I would have been familiar with what partying—or pnp—meant: doing crystal meth and "playing." But I, even at my most promiscuous, tended to stick to the guys who were most like myself, just your average-Joe types, guys who'd been to college, guys who could pass for straight, guys who came over clean and whose tastes always, always ran toward the vanilla.

For whatever reason, the night of JD, I wanted something different.

Maybe I was becoming jaded.

Maybe the wholesome dudes didn't do it for me anymore.

So I told JD I partied a bit and invited him over. The moment I'd given him my address and phone number, I started having misgivings. I remember I even typed out a text to him, saying something had come up and I'd have to call things off.

But I never sent it.

There was part of me that wanted everything that happened.

When he arrived, I was still keyed up, nervous. When I saw this wild, sweaty guy who was still cute despite the obvious signs of drug abuse, I again wondered if there was a way I could get out of things.

But I persisted. Something kept me relentlessly marching forward.

Even when he brought out the pipe.

Even when he tried to fist me. By the way, it didn't happen!

Even when I had an inkling he was stealing. I wasn't so stupid, I realize now, that I didn't have some idea he was up to no good. I knew! I just didn't want to admit it to myself—because that would make me, in a way, complicit. It would make me a fool for even letting him in the door in the first place, ignoring the million or so red flags that flapped in my face throughout our whole encounter, beginning with our online time.

Plus...I was afraid of him. Afraid of what he might do if I confronted him. Now, mind you, I didn't notice the extent of what he'd stolen from me that night until he was gone. In fact, it took days to find things I just assumed were there, weren't. I didn't notice they were missing until I needed them and went looking for them, which was probably something he counted on.

And... This is something I hate to admit, because it makes me sound so weak. But in spite of the drugs, the edgy appearance, the stealing, there was something inherently sweet about him and about that night. Isn't that shocking? How pathetic does it make me to even think that? Sweet? For Christ's sake!

It sounds crazy, I know, but there was this need for love that radiated off him. We had lots of sex that night, sure, but what I really remember is how late in the night, when the rest of the world had gone to sleep, he wanted so badly to simply be held. To lie in my arms with his head on my chest.

That image is so at odds with everything else, it leaves me perplexed.

I could practically taste his hunger—not for sex but for closeness, warmth, and human connection.

And now, as I think of it, it brings tears to my eyes.

Jimmy's nothing more than a little boy lost, trying to find his way.

I turn over in bed and stare at the wall. In spite of this realization, I doubt I can forgive. And I certainly doubt I could ever trust.

I slip off into a troubled sleep, one with huge white clouds that part to reveal Jimmy's face.

His outstretched hand...pleading.

Chapter Eleven

JIMMY

Mangroves. It's a charming name, isn't it? Conjuring up images of white sand beaches along the Gulf Coast, oases of shade where you relish the sound of the surf and the aroma of briny saltwater-tinged air. Yeah, right...

So I'm in a place I swore I'd never set foot in again. But damn it, right now, what I need is this—a place without windows, a place that smells like bleach, come, and sweat, a place where darkness is untouched by the light of day outside, a place where tired electronica drones over the speakers nonstop. A place where it's endless night.

An alternate universe where men with only towels wrapped around their waists are permitted to go.

Yes, I'm at the baths. The one just east of downtown, where the Capitol Hill neighborhood is just beginning to take shape along its eastern slopes.

Mangroves.

I swore two years ago I'd never come back here because the baths are one gigantic trigger. I swear to God, 90 percent of the guys who check in at the little glassed-off office up front have meth and a pipe or a couple syringes secreted on their person as they inform the clerk of their preference for a room or a locker.

I used to spend a ton of time here, so much so all the help knew me. Most of the patrons did too.

I dealt here.

I even stole here. One of my biggest heists took place out of room 302. See, the walls here that surround all the little cubicles they call rooms don't even reach the ceiling. There's about a two-foot gap between the cubicle tops and the dusty, cobweb-infested ceiling. One night, or early morning really, I was super high and filled with good ideas. The place was close to empty when I managed to pull a bench from a common area up to the wall of a cubicle I knew was occupied by a fellow dealer, who just happened to be in the shower when I got inspired. I scrabbled up to the top and swung myself over and into his room, landing on the bed. I tore through his stuff quickly, breathing hard, one eye on the door, and before I knew it, I was heading out with about three thousand dollars' worth of meth, all his cash—another thou—and his iPad.

I didn't stick around that night to see if I'd be caught. I wasn't that high! I even had the presence of mind and the good sense not to set foot in the place again for the following month.

I was lucky. I was suspected but never caught. Not really.

But people began to distrust me after that. My credibility dropped. How much credibility does a meth-head, drug-dealing slut have anyway?

I just didn't care.

I was too high almost all the time. And I kept myself busy, texting boys who were looking for a gram or more and those who were cruising online for sex. There was an endless supply!

It seems like the life of a different person now. Sometimes when I look back at my recent past, it's like a movie unspooling in my head. It doesn't even seem real, except as a story that happened to someone else.

Except it doesn't. Not when I'm sitting here at Seattle's oldest—and filthiest—bathhouse.

Why, it's like I've come home!

I've taken the cheapest room on the menu. There's a single bed. Next to it there's a particleboard cube that serves as a nightstand. The room's décor is completed by a gray locker, rusting along the bottom. A mirror clings to the wall opposite the bed, reflecting all that charm back. There's no monitor for watching porn—I don't have the cash for that upgrade. The linoleum floor's gritty against my bare feet. I shudder to think of the bacteria that's probably blossoming on its surface. Don't even get me started on the mattress!

In the room next to me, I can hear a guy getting fucked. How do I know? Because he's practically screaming things like "Yeah! Fuck me harder!" and "Breed me, man!"

Charming, right? A real Hallmark moment.

Right now, I'm curled up on one side, legs drawn up to my chest. I came here all fired up to say *fuck it* and simply use again. I could practically feel the rush of the drug in my veins as I bounced from foot to foot at the check-in window, waiting for my towel and my room key. I had decided. I had flipped that switch. I was going to use again. The hell with two years sober! What had it really gotten me anyway?

Right then, a little oblivion, a little escape, sounded just perfect. A ticket to bliss.

It wasn't until I got to this tiny room, with its stiff white sheets and its disinfectant smell, and closed the door behind me that I drew in a deep breath to quell my pounding heart and wondered: *What the hell am I doing here?*

In spite of the question, I took off my clothes and hung them in the locker. I locked it and wrapped the key, on a springy bracelet, around my bicep.

And then I tied the towel around my middle and sat on the bed. I simply stared for the longest time at my reflection in the mirror.

The guy looking back at me was not the same guy I used to see in mirrors around this joint. It wasn't just my physical difference—now there was more weight, short hair its natural color, piercings removed—it was the whole vitality thing.

Even in the dim and dingy light of the room, I could see my eyes were bright. My skin was clear. Back in the day, I had sores all over. I never knew what they were but assumed they were from the drug, which sweated out through my pores. I called 'em speed bumps. But today I exuded a kind of energy. A kind of light.

Eventually, I had to turn away from myself. Looking at the way I am now was like a reprimand. It was too painful a reminder of how far I'd come.

How could I go through with this if I had to look at this handsome, wholesome boy? How could I do this to him? Someone I'm supposed to love…

So I lay down and turned to the wall, which is where I now find myself, trying not to hear the pounding taking place next door. Trying to shut out the dank smell that seems to have seeped into every surface in this hellish place.

I know what I *should* be doing, what I *imagined* doing as I walked over here. It was what I had done thousands of times before. You cruised the two floors of the place, looking for open doors. Guys waited in those rooms, and many, many of them had little glass pipes hidden, along with tiny glassine bags filled with shards. I visualized those things as I made my way here, saw them the same way a thirsty man in the desert pictures an oasis.

But then I got here, in this tawdry little room, and I knew how it would go.

The fact that I would find someone who was partying, even though it was a weekday during the day, was certain. As I mentioned, there was always someone partying at Mangroves. It was party central. When I was dealing, I could walk out of here after a weekend with thousands of dollars in my pocket. As long as I had product, people bought.

The "candy man," someone once called me.

Now all I needed to do was go into a guy's room, maybe make a little small talk, maybe not. Because really all that needed saying was *Are you partying?* And we'd be off to the races. If they weren't, I'd just move on. The next guy, or the guy after that, was sure to be holding.

And then I'd bring the pipe to my lips, fire it up with most likely some sort of butane lighter, and watch as the glass bowl filled with lovely clouds of white smoke. Draw it in; exhale it into the air.

Even thinking of it now fills me with a paradoxical need and dread—all at the same time. This potent mix of want/not want is what has me immobilized, lying here on this bed in a fetal position, actually contemplating sucking my thumb.

God, it's been years!

But old habits stick around. They're always inside us, just below the surface. We only need to reach in deep to access them.

A part of me urges *Get out of here. Go home. It's not too late.*

And another part feels like that idea would all but kill me. Leaving is an intolerable notion.

What am I going to do?

How can I leave? How can I stay?

Do what you came here for, a seductive voice says. *One time isn't going to hurt anything. One lousy time—you deserve that much.* It's not so much the words that get me to my feet; it's the need. A need that, once awakened, can't be denied.

I cross to the door, open it.

Things have gone quiet next door. The door opens, and a swarthy man, completely naked, sweaty, emerges and hurries by, his eyes cast down at the dirty carpeted floor.

Someone moves at the end of the hallway, and I jump a little when I realize it's my own reflection in a mirror.

I stare at myself and realize I'm just another dude at the baths. *Go on. Get you some.*

On the second floor, I find a likely prospect. The room is dim, but a skinny guy with a Mohawk and too many tats lies prone on the bed, a damp towel thrown loosely over his dick and balls. He has a septum piercing. His ribs stick out. He's got one of the rooms with a video monitor, and even though the sound is muted, the screen casts flickering light upon him. He eyes me warily and plays with what's under the towel in a bored way.

On the little table next to his bed is a tub of lube, a couple of cock rings, a pack of Marlboro Reds—even though city ordinance forbids smoking cigarettes indoors—and a pipe. He doesn't even bother trying to hide it.

My gaze narrows in on it, like my eyes are a camera with a sophisticated zoom lens. I can see the white residue, the black film at the bottom. I can taste the smoke in my mouth.

He motions with his head for me to come in.

I step in and stand there, paralyzed by want, paralyzed by a need to flee. My heart pounds.

"Close the door," he says in a husky voice.

I do.

I sit on the edge of the bed and watch as he loads a shard of Tina into the pipe's stem, tapping the top of it so it falls into the bowl. He hands me the pipe with a little cockeyed grin. He gropes under the bed and brings out a lighter. He gives that to me too.

I stare down for too long, my mouth suddenly dry, ice running through my veins, blood roaring in my ears so loud I can barely hear him when he asks, "You gonna hit that or what?"

Am I? Am I gonna *hit that*? I turn the pipe so the shard moves around inside. I imagine putting a flame to it, watching it as it turns first to a dirty liquid, then vapor, bringing it up to my mouth, drawing in...

I look in the mirror and see myself gripping the pipe. It's a vision I thought I'd never see again. When you get certain of something is when you're in trouble. "Just when you go thinking you're *clean*, that you're *cured*, is when you are absolutely not safe, sweetie," I hear Miriam say.

She must have been in that place of certainty when she swallowed all those Oxys that one afternoon and then got behind the wheel of her car.

Did she do it on purpose?

Did she see only one way out?

I turn the pipe in my hand, looking at it as though I expect it to come to life or something.

I have more than one way out. I know that.

I glance up in the mirror again and see *not* the skinny guy with the Mohawk at the other end of the bed, but Miriam. It jolts, almost as though a wave of electricity courses through me. She's just sitting there, knees together, designer purse clutched on her lap. She's wearing a pantsuit, and there's a patterned scarf wrapped around her neck. If she notices me staring, she gives no indication.

I drop the pipe. It bounces on the floor but doesn't break.

"Watch it, man!" The guy hops off the bed and scoops up the pipe. The towel around his waist slides to the floor. His ass is skinny and covered with sores. Did I ever find guys like this attractive?

He stares at me, clutching the pipe. "What the fuck, dude? You don't want to party, just say so."

I don't have to think. "I don't want to party."

I set the lighter back down on the bed. And then I stand and leave the room.

"Hey!" the guy calls. "You comin' back?"

I pause for just a second, waiting to see if he'll say more, trying to pull me into his web. But he doesn't. The door slams shut behind me. And I imagine him hitting the pipe. Alone. Because an addict always ends up alone.

I start toward my room, and as I go, my determination, my sense of liberation, increases with every step I take. A smile spreads across my face.

I feel like I've been holding my breath forever. Now I can breathe again.

I cannot get out of Mangroves fast enough. I dress quickly, head downstairs, and wait for the guy at registration to release me. I know we can never be sure of anything, but I'm as sure as I can be I won't be coming back here. This is a place for the dead, the walking dead… the waiting, the lonely.

As I press on the door that will take me from shadows into sunlight, my breath catches for my brothers inside. They're trapped. My heart goes out to them, wishing there was a way I could help ease them out of their chains, but no one knows better than I do that the key to unlock our chains is not in someone else's hands, but in our own.

Always.

Outside, a familiar face waits. He leans against one of the machines where you pay for parking, a look of concern in his dark eyes, arms crossed over his chest.

I don't say anything. I simply move toward him, and he takes me in his arms. He feels like skin and bones. But he's warm, and he smells clean. His faded flannel shirt is soft against my cheek. He strokes my hair. "Did you…?" We both know how that question ends.

I look up at him. He's not Miriam, but he's the next best thing. Because he cares. My roommate. My Kevin. In answer to his question, I simply shake my head.

"Good," he whispers and lets me go.

We say nothing for several moments as the traffic moves by us, east and west, and pedestrians pay us no mind. Two gay guys hugging on the sidewalk in Capitol Hill? Move along, folks, there's nothing to see here.

"How did you know I'd come here?"

Kevin closes his eyes for just a second, as though I've asked the stupidest question I could possibly blurt out. "C'mon, man. Where else would you go? Especially when you were such a fuckin' coward as to sneak out on me when I was in the shower. That was smooth." He shakes his head as he looks me up and down, but a grin plays about his lips in spite of the head shaking. It makes me feel loved.

"I could have gone lots of places," I say.

He shakes his head again. "No. I know you because I know myself. This place is where you'd come. It's where I'd come if I was lookin' to score. Ground zero for the tweaker." He pinches my cheek. Hard. "And that's not us, right?"

I nod.

"Right?"

"Yes. It's not us."

"You sure you didn't smoke a little, maybe? Just a taste? You need to be honest with me, Jimmy."

"I didn't, man. I swear."

He starts moving down the hill, steps purposeful. I follow.

"Why not?" he asks.

I think of Miriam, the incongruous image of her sitting in that shadowy, desperate bathhouse room. I don't think seeing her in that mirror was my imagination. She was there. My despair, my need for salvation, I believe, was so great in that moment that it called to her from wherever she is. Her light and love made it through—for just a second.

But a second was enough to change everything. A second was all I needed to really *see*. I heard someone say once that life changes in an instant. It can seem like change takes years, but those years are just building up to a moment of transformation.

I see Miriam again in my mind's eye, her dyed red hair and too-white teeth, her matronly designer clothes—and the sweet, sad kindness of her expression.

And for her, I want to drop to my knees right here on this sidewalk, in front of God and everyone, and give a great big heaving thanks. Because she cared. And she still cares.

I don't tell Kevin about Miriam, though. For one, he's too practical to go in for what he'd refer to as "hippy-dippy spiritual shit." For another, he's always been a little jealous of Miriam. He's always sort of been in her shadow. The former mentor versus the current one. He's stuck with being alive, being imperfect. He doesn't have this convoluted history of sweetness and tragedy—the woman who helped me beat my own demons but was unable to vanquish her own.

Kevin's just a guy. A guy, I realize now, in spite of our sort of makeshift existence, who loves me and cares about what happens to me. And he's something Miriam, sadly, was not: a survivor. He shows me that quality every day.

He cares. He loves me. Why else would he have been waiting for who knows how long outside Mangroves?

I stop him with a hand on his shoulder, forcing him to look at me. I want to give his question the most honest answer I can. "I realized, almost too late, what I was throwing away."

He nods.

"And I knew one thing—my need to use was not as strong as my need not to."

He continues on down the street, talking out of one corner of his mouth. "Well, that's a lot of twelve-step bullshit, but it'll do because it has the ring of truth. I think there's more to it than that, and maybe someday, when you're ready, you'll tell me what the more is."

For just a second, I think about spitting it all out. The vision, everything.

But then he says, "You hungry?"

And I realize I'm starving. I haven't touched a morsel since last night's dinner, and I feel depleted—for many reasons, food being just one of them. My belly growls as though to answer Kevin.

We laugh. "Yup," I say. "But we can't go to Becky's. I called in sick."

"Right. So no discount?"

"No discount."

"Shit. We got bologna and—"

I finish for him. "Doritos at home. No." I dig deep in the pocket of my jeans. I pull out a twenty and two ones, all crumpled. It's all the money I have to my name.

"I think I got enough to treat us to Happy Meals."

"That would make me happy," Kevin says, quickening his pace. There's a McDonald's about three blocks away, but isn't that always the case?

I look at him ahead of me and think sometimes just the act of being there for someone else is enough. But I also bring to mind the fact that he was waiting—and would have waited for who knows how long—for me to come out. He would have given me a hug either way, no matter what choice I'd made.

"Me too! Starving," I say, catching up.

We'll eat and we'll figure out what to do. That's what life is all about, right?

Right?

Friday

Chapter Twelve

MARC

Should I go in to work?

A little voice inside, or maybe it's the devil on my shoulder, tells me I deserve a three-day weekend. Just three days to loll around my apartment, feeling sorry for myself that yet another venture into love has come to naught. I can eat chocolate and ice cream, drink vodka straight from the bottle, binge-watch old black-and-white weepers on Netflix, drown in my sorrow. Commiserate with other losers at love. Hello, Bette Davis.

It seems to be the path I'm doomed to follow where romance is concerned.

Will I end up an old queen, like Don, alone and bitter, with only a couple of pets to keep me company? It's sad that I can visualize that future a bit too clearly.

But no! I shake my head. From all indications, Don isn't unhappy. He loves his cats! He seems to enjoy living single. "I can drink vodka and eat ice cream in my underwear in the middle of the night if I want to, and there's no one to tell me it's bad," he's told me on more than one occasion. Funny how our perceptions of ice cream and vodka differ—and how that perception makes all the difference between happiness and despair. Here's me, too judgy, always thinking *how pathetic*, but maybe he has a point. And maybe his freedom is exactly his highest and best good—for him.

Who am I to judge?

Okay, so maybe Don's life isn't all that bad. But I know it isn't for me. I know I don't want to end up alone.

And yet this latest experience, this last time at bat, where I made myself vulnerable once again and got bitten for it, makes me wonder if real love will ever happen. I'm pushing forty, as I never cease to stop reminding myself. I go out sometimes to bars on the weekends, and I notice being *not* noticed the way I used to. I may kid myself that I don't, but in my heart of hearts, I know it's true. I don't get the same number of looks I used to. Those admiring glances, the smiles, the little flirts I used to take for granted are getting fewer and farther between. Maybe that's why I often tell myself I'm too tired to go out, that what I really want to do is stay in, pop some popcorn, and catch up on what's recorded on my DVR.

When the truth is: going out, more and more, feels like an exercise in vanishing, in invisibility. Why didn't anyone tell me that's what happens to gay men as we age? We become invisible.

Well, I'm certainly making a good case for calling in and staying home and feeling sorry for myself! Later I can call Pagliacci and order in pizza. I can drift in and out of sleep and imagine that perfect man I'm never able to find. Perhaps I'll hug a couple of pillows close to me and pretend they're my dream man.

No. Feeling sorry for myself is not the answer. If I *am* going to make a three-day weekend out of it, I'm not going to waste it.

Even if I don't follow Don's advice to get under a man, I will put myself out into the world. I will hike Discovery Park. Or drive over to the Olympic Peninsula and wander around in the rain forest I've always heard about but never seen. Or if I don't feel like being outside, I'll check out the movies on offer at the Sundance Cinema over in the University District.

I'll treat myself well, because if I don't, who will?

And there I go again...

I shake my head. I'm just a silly old fool. I might as well go to work. After all, why use up a personal day when I'm feeling blue? Save it for when I'm happy.

I get up from bed and open my bedroom window blind. At least today is in better sync with my mood. Gray clouds mass over Lake Union, obscuring the Cascades in the far distance. Strands of fog swirl just above the water so the houseboats across from me, hugging the shore of the Eastlake neighborhood, are almost hidden—just dark geometric shapes on the water. A couple of rowing shells cut through the lake. I envy them their freedom, knowing right down to my core that they're blissfully happy, just like everyone else.

Except me.

And there I go again. I'd laugh about my self-pity if it weren't so, well, sad.

I look at the clock and see that it's almost eight. I slept right through my phone's alarm, or shut it off with no recollection. I've done it before.

Whatever. No one at Panorama Healthcare, other than Don, pays much attention to when I arrive, when I leave, how long I'm gone for lunch. As long as I'm not missing deadlines, as long as I answer e-mails—which I can do from my iPad, right here in bed!—I don't think most of my coworkers think twice about where I am or what I'm doing.

I guess some people would perceive this as the ideal job. But today it just adds to that feeling I was musing over earlier—being invisible.

I get up and slide into my robe. It's chilly. The thermostat in the bedroom reads a cool sixty-five. I shut the window and turn the heat up. I start to head out to get myself some breakfast when I remember my phone. I'm curious if there will be evidence on the home screen of an alarm having sounded.

I trudge back to retrieve it from my nightstand. And I immediately see there's a partial text.

From Jimmy. Or JD. Or whatever the fuck he wants to call himself.

Just seeing that he's been in touch, while I slept, makes my heart skip a beat, makes me catch my breath. I care more than I want to admit, I realize.

Please. Can I talk to you? Just talk...

I press the Home button, key in my code, and go to text messages, my mouth suddenly dry. It almost feels like he's in the room with me, watching.

I think about just deleting the message without even seeing the rest of it. But I can't do that.

Please. Can I talk to you? Just talk is all I ask, Marc. I want to try to explain some things. And yeah, even though I know I don't deserve even the courtesy of your attention for five minutes, I hope you'll give it to me. I'm kind of an optimist that way.

Anyway, if you want, come by the diner for breakfast soon. Your meal's on me.

I wonder how much talking we could do when he's busy at the diner. And then I wonder why I'm wondering such a thing.

Are you really contemplating hearing him out? Seriously? What does that say about you?

I shake my head. Why should I do that much for him—give him that much consideration?

I consider deleting the message. In fact, my finger is poised to swipe so that it's gone, but then I sigh and just leave it there.

I head for the shower.

*

As I head south for work on the bus, I get an idea. A crazy, mean, stupid idea.

I pull the cord for the bus stop at Mercer, and I get off and start walking west on one of Seattle's busiest thoroughfares. This route will take me to Becky's Diner in lower Queen Anne. I had a similar urge recently, except then I was contemplating the age-old dilemma of eggs or pancakes. Sweet or savory?

What I'm contemplating this morning, though, is neither sweet nor savory.

It's bitter.

It's mean.

It's beneath me.

And as the traffic swarms by in a river of fumes, glass, chrome, and metal, I smile. I don't care if it's beneath me. I don't care if I hurt him.

He deserves it.

I silence the little voice inside me, the one that says *You're above this*, and continue on my way. I should be to Becky's in fewer than ten minutes. I let my rage carry me forward, my sense of indignation and betrayal. There's a kind of mad joy in it.

When I arrive, Jimmy sees me immediately. He grins, and I spy something—relief maybe—course through him. He gives a small wave, which I do not return.

From my experience, I know he waits on tables. Behind the long counter, with its red pleather and chrome stools, a heavyset woman with a kerchief, tattoos, and a raspy voice holds sway over the few people—all men—gathered at the counter. Most of them are sipping coffee, eating, or reading tablets or old-school newspapers.

I join them.

I smile at the woman, and she smiles back. She's kind of pretty in a sort of Seattle hipster way, with dyed black hair underneath the kerchief, a nose ring, and a piercing just above her upper lip that makes me wonder how she ever removes it.

By way of greeting, she arrives quickly with a glass carafe of coffee. To minimize confusion about the nearly black beverage inside, she holds it up and declares, "Coffee."

Obviously, there's no choice in the matter, so I turn over the cup in front of me and slide it toward her. She fills it and sets a menu down. She taps its plastic surface. "The blueberry pancakes are especially good today."

I stare down at it. Suddenly my face burns, and I feel this great wave of emotion rise up. I have a little trouble identifying it, even as it's making me sweat, making it hard to breathe, making me feel like I could burst into tears. Blueberry pancakes—or any food, for that matter—sound disgusting.

How stupid I am!

I gulp some of the coffee, and it's way too hot. Pain radiates out from my mouth and throat, like needles. I wish I could spit it out, but I'm much too decorous a fellow for that.

The menu blurs before me, which is a good thing, because I don't think I've ever been less hungry in my entire life. If I could see what else is on offer, the omelets, the French toast, the skillets, I think I'd puke. I shove it away and lift the coffee cup again. My hands tremble, and I spill some. It doesn't burn me, but it splatters on the white button-down shirt I put on this morning.

Just to make everything worse, Jimmy comes up to me. At my shoulder, he whispers into my ear, his breath warm, "Hey."

I peer at him out of the corner of my eye.

"There's a booth that just opened up. You want it?"

I glance over his shoulder, avoiding his gaze, and look as though to verify he's not lying to me.

"Nah. I'm good here." Even though I don't want to peruse it, I slide the menu back over in front of me and begin my best effort to focus. I call to the woman manning the counter, heedless of being rude, "Can I get a number three?" A number three is three eggs, three bacon slices, three sausage links, toast, and cottage fries.

I'm quite certain I couldn't swallow one bite of it.

I stare desperately at the waitress, hoping she can read my mind and understand that I'm trying to separate myself from this guy at my shoulder.

She simply glares at me and nods. I don't blame her. She's in the middle of taking another customer's order.

"C'mon, Marc, I'll take care of your order. Did you get my text? Breakfast is on me this morning."

I allow myself just a fraction of a second to meet his eyes. And what I read there almost breaks my heart. It's such vulnerability, such a need to connect.

I am not this stoic man who can harden himself to earnest and entreating looks like the one Jimmy's giving me right at this very moment.

I call out to the counter woman, who I'm sure I'm pissing off more and more, "Can I get that to go? I gotta get to work!"

Jimmy says, "What's your problem?"

I turn and force myself to look at him for longer this time. Part of me wants to fling my scalding coffee in his face.

And the other?

The other wants to kiss him.

Both are as irrational as hell.

The dark-haired woman behind the counter finally moseys over. She's smiling and continues to smile broadly as she delivers the following:

"Look. I don't know who you think you are or what you think I am to *you*, but you order when it's your turn. When I come up to you with a smile like this one—" She pauses to point up at her face. I notice how red her lipstick is and how she reminds me suddenly of that old screen siren Bettie Page. "—then you place your order. You wait your turn. Or you can get the fuck out of here."

"It's okay, Erma. He's here to see me," Jimmy says. He's smiling and wringing his hands, hopping from one Converse-clad foot to the other. He touches my shoulder. "Come on, man. Come to the booth."

Someone behind him calls, "Can I get more coffee over here, please?"

Jimmy looks nervously behind him. "Right away," he answers.

"I gotta work," he tells me. "I missed yesterday, and I'm gonna get my ass fired. So would you please, please sit yourself down in that booth over there?" he pleads. "I have a break coming up, and we can talk then. Okay?"

All I can do is shake my head. Words elude me. I reach into my pocket, pull out a ten, and fling it on the counter. "Erma?" I call. "I'm sorry."

And I hurry from the diner, wondering if the bigger shitheel in this pair of shitheels—Jimmy and me—isn't actually me.

Chapter Thirteen

JIMMY

I watch Marc go. He rushes out the door as though I have something contagious, as if he can't stand to even breathe the same air.

I wonder why he showed up here at all. The optimist in me thought he'd at the very least wanted to talk, wanted to hear my side of things.

But reality calls for a more pessimistic view.

"Hey! Waiter! How about that coffee?" The guy in the third booth from the door calls out again, reminding me of the duties at hand. I go grab the pot from behind the counter and approach the table, refill his cup.

With a lot of sarcasm, he says, "Thank you *so much.*"

"Sorry about that." I give him one of my most contrite smiles, but it seems lost on him. As though I wasn't even there, he goes back to staring at the book he's reading after making sure I knew I was doing a lousy job of taking care of my customers.

I check on my other tables, asking everyone if their food is okay. I take note of a couple of requests for checks. I go to the back to tally them up, and while doing that, I let myself recall the question of why Marc came in here.

Maybe it was to punish me? To make me see what my actions cost me? What I missed out on?

Who knows? I bring booth four and six their checks and tell them to pay Erma up front at the cash register.

Maybe I should just let him go. If he did indeed come in here to make me feel bad, he succeeded, but he also showed himself to not be as nice of a person as I thought he was. I know that's a shitty thing for me to think of him, especially after all the stuff I inflicted on him, both two years ago and in the present, but there it is.

Maybe thinking he's not worth it is my way of minimizing the pain I know is waiting in the corner to pounce on me once I'm 100 percent certain, sure-as-sure as this optimist can be, that there isn't a snowball's chance in hell I'll get a second opportunity with him.

Distancing myself from him is a way of trying to undercut my future pain and the despair.

There's a quiet moment in the diner as the breakfast rush empties out. I stand behind the counter with Erma, who's a good kid, a fellow recovering addict who's been clean for more than a decade. I look up to her.

"What was with that guy?"

I pretend I don't know what she's talking about. "What guy?"

She punches me in the arm—hard. Erma's a take-no-shit kind of gal. "You know what guy. He looked like you were about to molest him or something. You should have seen his face. It wavered between looking totally sick and absolutely petrified." She grins. "What did you do to him?"

I grin back. I am *not* going to fill her in. Like I'm kidding, I say, "If you only knew."

I get busy helping her refill salt and pepper shakers. "He's just a guy. We went out a couple of times."

She shakes her head. "He's not *just a guy*. Even this confirmed single gal can see you feel something for him."

I cock my head.

"Oh yes, Jimmy. I'd have to be blind not to see how into him you are."

"And I don't get that." I confirm her impression. "We've only been together a few times."

"Oh, honey." She finishes up with the salts and peppers and loads them onto a tray for me to dispense to the booths. "I hate to go all bad romance on you, but caring about someone isn't always measured in length of time. You can be with someone for forty years and it still might not be right. Trust me. I know. My parents got divorced *after* they retired." She chuckles, but there's little mirth in the laughter. "And some people fall in love within minutes of laying eyes on someone else." She winks. "It's a scientific fact. Look it up."

I take the tray and start setting out the salt and pepper shakers, thinking about what Erma said. Was it love at first sight? Not when he was in here the other day for breakfast, but that night I spent with him two years ago?

Back in those days, I stole from lots of tricks. And I couldn't wait to get away from them. But with Marc, I wanted to stay, even if the notion was absurd. I mean, here I was sneaking his stuff into my empty backpack every time he trustingly left the room.

And yet... I remember lying on the bed with him. I was high and guilty because he truly seemed like this nice and vulnerable guy. Sweet.

I just wanted him to hold me.

That sounds crazy. But it's true.

I felt something for him. Maybe, like Erma says, the moment I laid eyes on him. But I was too high, too warped to recognize love at first sight when it came up and tweaked my nose. Maybe that's why I never forgot him.

Oh, why didn't he forget *me*?

Erma's right. What she saw on my face standing at Marc's shoulder was real. Was it love? I don't know for sure, but I still want to find out.

The bell above the door jingles, and I look up to see someone enter. There's a guy about my own age standing there, and everything about him screams *tweaker*. I know all the signs—the oily, sweaty skin, the kind of crazed look in his eyes, like they're bugging out, the way he restlessly shifts his weight from one foot to the other. He looks at the counter, the booths, me, Erma, as though his gaze can't seem to find a place to land.

Erma, quick at sizing people up, calls to him. "The bar's to the right."

He doesn't thank her, just heads off to the bar portion of the diner, which is almost completely separate from the eating section.

"That boy is fucked up," she whispers as I return to the counter.

"No kidding." I suddenly feel something for this character I've only seen for about a minute. Sadness. That feeling I had when I left the baths—that some of those inside were trapped.

He could have been me.

After a while, a few more people start to filter into the restaurant, early lunch, late breakfast. There's what I assume is a lesbian couple, one with spiky bleached-blonde hair with pink highlights and the woman I assume is her wife or girlfriend, a stunning brunette who reminds me of Katy Perry. An older man, a regular named Joe, takes his usual spot at the counter with his usual book, *Watership Down*, which I swear he's been reading through his little round rimless glasses for years—or at least ever since I've worked here. I don't know if he reads it over and over or is just a slow reader. Somehow, it seems rude of me to ask. There are a couple of guys, whom I get no gaydar off of, who take the booth at the very back and immediately pull out their phones and begin staring into their screens. Why bother to go out to eat together?

Through all this, and my attempting to put my all into serving the new rush of customers, I can't get my mind off the guy who came in an hour or so ago. I call him the tweaker. He stays with me because I think of Charles Dickens. Yes, Charles Dickens...and the Ghost of Christmas Past. Just a glimpse of that guy was like looking at myself in a mirror that has a magical ability to reflect the past.

I try to forget about him, but I can't. So when there's a lull in the flow of things, when everyone has their meals, their coffees, and their Cokes, I say to Erma, "I'm gonna take a little break."

"Need to smoke?"

"Something like that." It's funny. I haven't had a cigarette all morning, and even Erma's mention of smoking doesn't ignite any desire to do so. What I do have a desire to do is talk to the tweaker. I don't really understand the pull, which is almost irresistible. I'm hoping this urge is not a veiled way of tempting me—a trigger. I shrug.

I walk over to the bar side of the diner, and there he is, sitting hunched over a half-drunk tap beer. His thin fingers drum restlessly on the edge of the bar, and I notice how his one foot never stops moving, bouncing up and down on the perch at the bottom of his stool.

"What are you drinking?" I take a seat beside him and smile.

He looks at me like I'm a ghost, like I just appeared next to him out of thin air. He leans back, regarding me. "Do I know you?"

I lean close. "No. But I know you."

"What the fuck?" He musters up what I guess is his best dirty look and then returns to staring into his beer.

"So, what are you drinking?"

"Mac and Jack's," he mumbles.

I motion toward Kyle, the bartender, "Bring this guy another Mac and Jack's. It's on me."

The tweaker stares at me. "Look, dude. I don't know what you're trying to pull, but I'm not in the market for any action." He sizes me up, looking me up and down. "Especially not of the gay variety."

Kyle sets his new beer before him. I watch as the tweaker drains the first and starts in on my treat.

"You're welcome," I say.

He raises the glass to me while simultaneously rolling his eyes. "Thank you *very much.*"

Today seems to be my day for receiving sarcastic gratitude. I'll take it.

I lean closer. "Look, I'm at work, so I don't have much time, so I'll come to the point. Before, when I said I knew you, it was because I know myself, and I see a lot of me in you."

"You're nothin' like me, man." He has some beer foam clinging to his upper lip. He wipes it away with his finger.

"Not so much anymore, but once upon a time I was exactly like you. Always sweaty, couldn't stay still…"

"I'm the nervous type," he says. He takes another sip of the beer, stares down at the bar. I notice how he tenses—his shoulders rise, hunching up.

"Yeah, right. I think we have a friend in common. Goes by the name of Tina?"

He puts down his beer and turns to me, allowing himself a brief eye connection. "I don't know what the fuck you're talking about."

"Yes, you do." I just let the words lay there for a minute or so. I'm not sure what I expected from this encounter or why I felt compelled to reach out.

As the silence stretches out, I think how I need to be getting back to the other side, to the tables I know will now need my attention.

I'm about to throw a couple of bills down on the bar for the tweaker's beer when he says something to stop me.

"Yeah, you do." He shrugs. "What are you? Some kind of undercover cop? You part of some sting operation? Because if you think you're fooling me, you're not. I see you parked outside my crib—or someone like you, watching me all the time."

Ah, the tweaker paranoia. Classic. I'd almost forgotten about it. Once I used to think my neighbors were piping in voices through my radiator.

"Right, I'm an undercover cop who just happens to work as a waiter, and the waiting I do is in the hopes that some guy, high on T, will stroll into my clever trap, and I can arrest him." I chuckle at the scenario, but he doesn't. He merely looks uncomfortable.

"You're not a cop? You have to tell me, you know."

"I'm not."

"Are you sure? Because—"

I cut him off. "Will you listen to yourself? That shit is making you crazy. I know because I've been crazy like you."

Erma peeks into the bar. Our gazes connect. She crooks a finger at me to come hither. She's not smiling.

I touch his arm and am relieved that he doesn't pull away. "Look, I gotta get back to my job." I add, by way of reassurance, "You know, my job waiting tables? Anyway, I'll be done in a couple hours. Maybe we could talk after."

He doesn't say anything and has resumed his position of staring down at the bar's dark wood surface.

When I get up, he looks up at me and I can see his eyes are glossy—like unshed tears stand in them. "You look just like my brother."

I cock my head. "What?"

"Nothin'." The connection breaks.

"I gotta get back to work, but if you wanna hang and just talk a little bit more, I'll be done soon."

He only shrugs. I think I've done all I can do here and head back to what I know will be some very impatient customers.

*

Later, when my shift's over, I go and look for the tweaker, but he's no longer in the bar. Nor is he in the restroom.

I'm disappointed and don't quite understand why. I should have figured he wouldn't stick around to talk to a creepy dude like myself, sticking my nose all up in his business. After all, what's it to me if he's acquainted with Tina? He probably assumes I was either looking to score or hit on him. Still, I feel a certain sense of loss when I realize he's not waiting. It's been a hell of a day for loss, for disappointment, from the get-go.

When I step outside, he's standing under our front awning, an unlit cigarette hanging out of his mouth. He eyes me warily and then approaches.

The cigarette bounces up and down in his mouth as he asks, "Gotta light?"

I pull out my own smokes and the disposable lighter in my pocket. I hold it out to him. He takes it, lights up, and the smoke, a cloud, seeps out around the cigarette and through his nostrils.

I'm still addicted to this stuff. The sight of him, the smell propels me, almost as though I have no say in the matter, to ape him.

I exhale smoke and look at him. "Glad you stuck around."

Smoking, he stares out at the busy street in front of us. More to the passing traffic than to me, he says, "I don't know why. I got other things to do."

"Oh yeah? Like what?"

His gaze cuts back to me, and he raises his eyebrows. He sighs, shrugs. "Nothin'." He continues to smoke for a while and then says, "Nothin' at all. Story of my life."

"I think I know that story." I start to walk away from the restaurant. "Take a walk with me?"

He eyes me warily. "What for?"

I stop. "Look, dude. I'm not trying to hook up with you. I'm not hoping for a hit off that pipe you have in your pocket."

His eyes widen, and his mouth drops open.

"I just wanna talk to you." It occurs to me that if he's going to ask why, I'm not sure I have an answer ready. I don't know what fuels my compassion here, my need to connect with this stranger, but the intention, the will, is so strong I can't say no to it.

He shrugs and follows me without a word.

We head through the busy streets of lower Queen Anne. I let my feet guide us. Through no real conscious decision of my own, I find myself leading him up Queen Anne Hill. Let me tell you, the path I've chosen is a steep motherfucker, straight up for close to a mile.

Halfway up, I notice the difference in our breathing, in our whole demeanor. I'm huffing and puffing a bit—because of the smoking, I'm sure—and my heart's pumping at double time, but I feel pretty good, actually. Energized.

But the tweaker demonstrates the difference between a habitual user of crystal meth and one who's been off the stuff for two years.

He's panting. He can barely catch his breath. Sweat rolls down his face. He's taken off the beat-up and filthy denim jacket he wore, and the pale blue T-shirt underneath is dark with sweat under his arms. A circle of sweat stain even blooms outward from his chest and around his collar. Add all this to the fact that it's gray and overcast and probably only about, at best, fifty-one degrees out.

He notices me noticing. "What are you tryin' to do? Kill me?" he gasps.

"Sorry. I just want to get us up to Kerry Park." Saying our destination out loud informs me as much as it does him. "We can admire the view."

"Really? Even if I'm dead?"

I laugh. "C'mon. You can make it. You're a young guy."

He gives me a dirty look. But we soldier on. Upward.

Once we get up to Kerry Park, on Highland Avenue, we collapse on a bench. Because it's a weekday in the middle of winter, we have the park to ourselves, save for what appears to be a straight couple at the other end of the park, taking selfies with the gorgeous view as their backdrop.

The view from up here is one of the best in a city full of breathtaking views. From where the tweaker and I sit, the whole of downtown Seattle, the Space Needle, the ports, and what seems like all of Puget Sound spread out before us. It's almost unreal, like a backdrop some movie art director set up.

Mount Rainier, because of the clouds, is the only landmark hidden from view. I watch as a couple of ferries cut through the slate-gray waters of Elliott Bay.

"You got a smoke?" he asks.

I finger the pack and the lighter in my pocket. "Seriously? After all that, you want a cigarette?" I chuckle. "Dude, you're suicidal." I contemplate giving him one because I kind of want another myself, but I shake my head. "Sorry. All out."

He looks bereft. I mean, not just disappointed, but completely crestfallen. Almost like he's about to start crying. Should I relent and feed his nicotine addiction? Is it *that* bad? "Dude, it's not the end of the world. We can get more up on the hill. There's a 7-Eleven."

He seems to be engaged with the panorama before him and neither speaks nor looks at me for the longest time. Out of the corner of my eye, I watch him and notice the emotion clouding his features. I can see that under the sallow and slick complexion, the greasy hair and dirty clothes, there's a handsome young man. Again, I think of myself and how I once was and how easily I could be him again.

At last he turns to me, and I see the tracks of tears on his face. "What's your name, anyway?"

"Jimmy."

He doesn't extend a hand for me to shake, but he tells me his name—Frasier.

"Like the guy on TV?"

"Yeah." He nods. "*Just* like the guy on TV." He snorts, and I relax a bit against the bench, glad I could make him laugh.

"You remind me of my brother," Frasier says.

"Yeah? In what way?"

He shrugs. "You look a lot like him. That is, before he got into this crap." He gropes in his pocket and pulls out his little glass pipe, stained with white residue and black on the bottom of the bowl. He looks around guiltily and slides it back in his pocket.

"He was a tweaker too?"

"Yup. He gave me my first taste."

I close my eyes, and a wave of sadness washes over me. I think about the irony of his brother looking like me before he got into Tina and how I am now, *post* Tina—I hope. I should tell Frasier the truth. "I used to be a tweaker, too, man."

"I figured. You want a hit?" He slides his hand back into his pocket. He turns to look over his shoulder, searching, presumably, for a less public place for us to retire to where we can smoke up in peace.

I'd be lying if I said I wasn't tempted to throw caution to the wind and fire up what's left in that pipe right here in Kerry Park. But I say, "Nah. I don't do that stuff anymore. But I used to be into it pretty heavy." I even tell him I graduated to slamming—or injecting—toward the end. "I dealt that shit too. Only way I could afford my habit, once upon a time."

"Wow. You'd never know it to look at you." He eyes me up and down, taking inventory. "You look too wholesome. I had you pegged as some former frat boy at UDub." He chuckles. I notice him fingering the pipe in his pocket.

This reference to fraternities and the University of Washington makes me laugh. I don't think anyone's ever used the word *wholesome* in the same breath with me before. I tell him that.

He shakes his head. "You look like the most powerful shit to ever cross your lips is maybe a couple beers on the weekend."

"That's funny. I don't even drink beer anymore."

"Good for you."

We're quiet for a while, just two guys sitting on a bench, enjoying the view. Well, it's pretty to think so, anyway.

At last I ask, "Why? Why do you do it?"

"That's a good question, especially in light of my bro." He gnaws on his lower lip.

"Why? What happened to him?"

"Dead."

It jolts me.

Frasier goes on. "He committed suicide. Jumped off the Aurora Bridge, back before they put up the extra fencing to keep people from doing that."

I think, of course, of Miriam and how she died on the very same bridge.

Frasier lets out a breath, a shaky, trembling gasp edging on sobbing. "It was the shit that drove him to it, you know? He wanted to quit, man. Tried so *fuckin'* hard too." He laughs, but there's no mirth in it. "I lost count of how many times he resolved to make the last time the *last* time; you know?"

I nod. "Oh yeah, I know."

"I think he threw himself off that bridge when he just realized there was no way out."

"And even with that, you still wanna get high?"

He pulls the pipe out again and lifts it, like a toast. "To his memory!"

"Put that away." I push his hand with the pipe down toward his pocket. "Don't you wanna get clean?" I draw in a breath, feeling my own rush of emotion rising up. "Don't you wanna be free?"

I expect him to scoff at me, maybe make fun, perhaps walk away.

But Frasier turns to me quickly and grabs me up in his arms. He's sobbing. This goes on for a couple of minutes, maybe more, and he doesn't say a word, just cries.

I cry too.

Finally he pulls away, and there's an intensity in our gazes as we look at each another. He smiles through his tears. "I do. I do. But I don't know how to get out of this mess. I'm just like him!" he moans. "I want to get away. I've tried. But I just can't."

I squeeze his shoulder. "You can," I say softly. "If I can, anyone can."

He shakes his head, and I anticipate him telling me it's impossible. It's what I would have said when I was in his shoes.

But he surprises me. "You're him, aren't you?" He touches my face.

"What do you mean?"

"You're Tommy. You look just like him. You even talk like him." He begins to sob again and puts his hand in his lap.

"Yeah," I nod. "I'm Tommy. And I love you too much to watch you make the same mistakes I did. Give me that pipe."

Without hesitating, he hands it over.

I get up and walk to the low fence that borders the park. The hill we're on drops sharply downward beyond the fence, and I raise my arm and fling the damn pipe as far as I can. I return to Frasier. "Baggie?" I hold out my hand.

He brings out a tiny pink glassine bag that looks way too familiar to me. I feel both longing and disgust inside me. There's very little left in there, some powder, one small rock. I return to the edge and open it, let its contents fly off in the wind. I move to a garbage bin and stuff the Baggie down deep inside it, under all the crap already in there.

I return to him. "There. You're free."

"It's that simple."

I nod, stop, and then shake my head. "You know it's not. But Tommy wants you to make this real." I nod and smile. "He's watching."

Frasier looks around, as though he expects to see his brother hiding behind a tree or a bush.

I pull out my phone and hold it in front of him, turning it. "You got one of these?"

He pulls his out. "Of course. Who doesn't?"

It still amazes me that even the poorest of the poor, these days, can manage to own a cell phone. But I recall what a lifeline one is when you're a druggie, even if you're homeless. I hold out my hand. "Give it to me." He does, and I input my own name, number, address, and e-mail in his contacts. I want him to have every avenue possible for contacting me, if he wants to. "I'm Jimmy. Not

Tommy. I'm here." I hand back his phone. "Remember that. Call me. You can come to a meeting with me. I'll help you. God help me, maybe I can even be your sponsor one day." I get up. "I have to go now, Frasier." I pause for a second and then say, "Brother." I smile. "I trust that you'll be in touch."

I start away. He calls, "Wait! Don't you want my number?" I stop, thinking about it, wondering if it's a good idea. I could call him if I don't hear from him. But at last I shake my head and say, "Eventually. But I wanna leave that first contact up to you. A very wise woman once told me that only one person holds the key to our freedom, and that's ourselves."

He nods. "I'll call you."

I smile. "No maybes."

"No maybes." He looks down at his phone screen. "I will."

"I believe you." I walk over to him. "Stand up." He does and I hug him, long and hard. He pulls away first.

"Wow. This was quite a coincidence, huh? Us running into each other? Thank you."

"You really believe that? That this was a coincidence?"

He's gnawing on his lower lip again. He says, "Nah."

I walk away. And this time I don't look back.

As I head down the hill, I hear the sound of a text come through. I pull my phone out and pause to look at the screen. I'm thinking maybe it's Frasier already.

But it's not.

It's Miriam.

You're a good person. You're worthy of love.

I gasp, and the screen blurs as tears fill my eyes. I blink and see that, of course, the message is not from her. How could it be? Kevin texted:

Ordering pizza for supper. You want in? I'll get a large.

I smile, suddenly famished.

You bet. With extra cheese and pepperoni, please.

I continue down the hill, grinning.

Saturday

Chapter Fourteen

MARC

Ah, the weekend and all its promise!

Once upon a time, I would have used this time for grocery shopping, the gym, laundry, and hooking up. Certainly not in that order! I might have even made time for other leisure activities, like reading, dining out, or watching movies, either at home or at one of my favorite cinemas around town.

There's something truly liberating about a Saturday, isn't there? Friday, with its promise, is but a memory, and Sunday, with its winding down and its dour peek toward the workweek, hasn't yet arrived. Saturday is the week's best foot, put forward.

I miss the freedom of Saturdays—especially today. Because today doesn't contain any of the joy of my other Saturdays. This one is an anomaly, a dark shadow, the bizarro-world opposite of what a Saturday is supposed to be. This one is a buzz kill, a real Debbie Downer.

I woke early but stayed in bed for hours after the dull, grayish sunlight seeping through my blinds ripped me from my slumber and my dreams. First, I simply contemplated those dreams and what they meant. I knew, from waking off and on all night, there had been many dreams, but the only one I remember when I wake fully is the last one, the one I interrupted with a snort and a sudden flipping up of my eyelids.

I felt a little disoriented, like my bed wasn't the place I was supposed to be, so I looked around myself suspiciously, heart beating hard, the back of my head damp with sweat. Everything was in its place, familiar—the David Hockney print in its black frame above my dresser, the silver-edged full-length mirror, propped against the wall opposite the bed, the black bookcase stuffed with the likes of Stephen King, Dean Koontz, Neil Gaiman, and Clive Barker. My nightstand was still next to the bed, with its chrome desk lamp, its stack of DVDs, some from Treasure Island Media, and a bottle of Wet, and, curiously, an ice cream scoop.

But it wasn't the catalog of surroundings that caused the uncomfortable tightness in my chest and the more rapid breathing.

It was the dream.

I'm there. Back to that damned night again. JD lies in bed next to me. His face is slick with sweat. His eyes can't seem to settle on anything. He keeps grabbing my arms and arranging them around himself. "Hold me," he whispers again and again, almost a litany, until the words themselves lose their meaning, until they're just urgent and demanding noises—the whimper of a wounded creature. I pull my arms away, attempting to get up from the bed, yet he grabs me, pulling my arms back around him in an approximation of a hug.

Shift.

JD's tying off his arm with one of my belts, eyeing me. In one hand he holds a syringe with a bright orange cap. "Vitamins," he tells me. "I need this to stay alive." But instead of plunging the needle into his arm, poking a vein, he removes the cap from the syringe with his mouth, spits it out, and jams the needle into his eye.

I jump back, feeling his warm blood splatter my face.

Shift.

He's at my front door, all dressed, the backpack bulging with all of my most treasured belongings—I know what's inside somehow. "I'll be back tonight to get everything else," he says.

Then he winks at me. "Including your heart."

The gesture would be sappy and romantic were it not punctuated by JD pulling a hunting knife from his pocket. He eyes me while giving its razor-sharp tip a quick lick, much as he had done to my cock when he first arrived hours ago.

That's when I wake. "Including your heart" echoes in my mind as I groggily sit up, taking stock, reassuring myself I'm not only in my own room, but in my own room alone.

It's the dream that keeps me in bed. Oh sure, I get up to answer the call of nature, always an early morning priority, but scurry back to the comfort of my flannel sheets, velour blanket, and quilt. It's almost like I'm afraid to get out of bed.

So I stay there, letting the hours tick by. I grab my iPad, check e-mail, look at Facebook, play a couple of games of Spider Solitaire. I grab the remote off the nightstand, wipe lube off it with the corner of the sheet, and turn the TV on. For an hour I watch, transfixed, an infomercial about an oven that will cook meat from its frozen state in record time.

And finally, around noon, I face myself—not only in the mirror across from the bed, but the pathetic self that lurks deep down inside. I can do this routine of self-denial and avoidance for only so long.

My dream was reminder enough that if someone is foremost in my thoughts, that someone needs to be reckoned with, one way or the other.

Even as I tell myself this, I'm getting up and reminding myself I need to eat. I shut down the brain, go in my kitchen, brew coffee, and make soft-boiled eggs and whole-wheat toast. I sit in front of my living room TV, eating, but don't look at its screen.

I stare morosely, chewing, at the view outside my sliders—the Cascade Mountains across the gray mirror surface of Lake Union. The clouds above the mountains are whitish-gray, dirty cotton balls. They remind me I'll get this day only once.

At last, after washing the dishes by hand even though I have a dishwasher, showering, shaving, flossing, brushing, doing a facial mask, dressing in flannel jogging pants and my favorite T-shirt—a black number with an abstract image of Grace Jones on the front—do I sit down and pick up the one item I've been avoiding all morning.

My phone.

I tap the Home button, key in my security code, and bring up my texts.

Nothing new, but the same one from Jimmy is still there.

Please. Can I talk to you? Just talk is all I ask, Marc. I want to try to explain some things. And yeah, even though I know I don't deserve even the courtesy of your attention for five minutes, I hope you'll give them to me. I'm kind of an optimist that way.

Anyway, if you want, come by the diner for breakfast soon. Your meal's on me.

I never did get that free breakfast, I think, a bitter smile turning up my lips at the corners. I shake my head and look at the clock on my DVR. It's after one now, too late for breakfast anyway. Besides, I already ate.

Hell, I think, *it's too late for lots of stuff.* Reconciliation. Forgiveness. Finding a man whom I might love. Learning to tap dance...

My head drops into my hands, almost like a cow lowering its head to graze. I can't leave it like this. Just like, way back when, I couldn't get JD and his thieving ways out of my head for at least a month after we met up, I know I won't be able to get Jimmy out of my head now either, not unless I can find some kind of resolution.

It dawns on me with stunning clarity that in my thoughts I refer to him as both JD and Jimmy, almost as though he's two different people.

And that's a profound thought. Because he is.

My mind, at the revelation, goes blank, like it simply shuts down for a few minutes. I close my eyes.

What am I supposed to do with this?

Oddly, Don's voice creeps into my head. *Why, sweetie, what you're supposed to do with it is act. You need to see the guy again, whether it's a first or last time or something in between, but you need to get things straight between you. You should pardon my use of the word! But really, honey, just talk to the man. There's something in the fact that you see him as two separate people.*

I shut Don up, much more easily than I could do if we were at work. I think that time and its simple passage will release me from my dreams and lack of closure surrounding JD/Jimmy. I can just let him go. Move on. Get under another man.

This last thought proves to me how wrong I am.

And without thinking about it, without allowing myself the time to censor, I snatch up my phone and reply to Jimmy's text.

Meet up? Tonight?

I don't want to be too nice, but I want to get this over with. Maybe then I can move on from this creature who has haunted my dreams for far longer than I want to admit, even to myself.

I set the phone back down on the coffee table. I take up the TV remote and access my DVR recordings. There's a *House Hunters International* on there, about a flight attendant buying herself a place in Sicily, I've been meaning to watch, and I sink into it.

I'd be lying if I said I wasn't listening for the sound of a text message coming through, a brief flash of my smartphone screen.

But I hear nothing back. I watch two more *House Hunter International* episodes, part of a movie with Sandra Bullock and Melissa McCarthy that fails to make me smile, let alone laugh, and two episodes of *Law & Order*.

Finally, just as the sky is beginning to darken, my phone speaks up, nudging me and informing me I have a text message. It's him.

Where at?

Do I dare invite him here? Uh, no. Remember how that worked out last time? Changed person or not, I'm not ready to invite him back to the scene of the crime.

Your place?

I wait, and within a couple of minutes:

Okay. 7:30?

I text him back a thumbs-up. I settle into the cushions of my couch, arms crossed over my chest, wondering what I'm letting myself in for.

Don pipes up again in my head. *A happy ending? Resolution? Disaster? Heartache?*

I whisper to myself, "Most likely—all of the above."

Chapter Fifteen

JIMMY

"Don't get your hopes up, bud," Kevin says to me as I sit, like a schoolgirl, with my hands folded in my lap on my twin bed.

"Hey," I caution him. "Marc's giving me a second chance."

Kevin nods and sits down beside me. "You're right about that. And that *can* be a good thing." He draws in a breath. "But a very wise person once told me that second chances aren't always about starting over. Sometimes they're about getting the ending right."

"You get that pearl of wisdom from a greeting card?"

He shakes his head slowly, looking deeply into my eyes. "Facebook."

We both crack up. But what he says is true. There was never any resolution between Marc and me about what happened a couple of years ago. Why would there have been? Who could have predicted we'd ever reach this juncture? When I left in the wee hours of that awful morning, as a person I look back at now and hate, I was certain I'd never see or hear from Marc again. In fact, I knew I'd ensure it.

So whatever happens tonight, if Marc does indeed show up, which I won't believe until I actually see him in front of me, is a crap shoot. I have to be ready for anything: anger, forgiveness, his never wanting to see me again—which I promise I will respect—reconciliation, disgust.

Anything can happen.

Which is why I'm sitting here right now, at a little past seven on a Saturday night, scared sick. And I mean that literally—my stomach is churning and gurgling. I haven't eaten anything since the meager makings I'd called lunch, a handful of stale peanuts and a Coke. I feel as though I can't move.

I'm so afraid of what may happen or what might not that it's left me in this no-man's-land which is very much like paralysis.

I wish he would just get here. I want the jitters to end. I need to know if there's a future or not. And yes, I realize Kevin and Miriam would *both* tell me the future is guaranteed to no one. Still, I can't stop myself from wishing the future would hurry up and get here.

I can't stand the suspense.

And just as that thought fires in my brain, our buzzer sounds. Kevin stands. "You want me to get that?"

I stand up, too, although to be honest, I'm feeling a little weak in the knees. I give Kevin what I know is a very sick grin. "Maybe this isn't such a good idea," I say suddenly, wondering how those words slipped from my lips. I plop back down on my bed. Ever since Marc left here the other night, I've been hoping and praying for this moment, so why would I say such a thing?

Kevin waves me away. "You just have stage fright. This is a good thing. You'll see."

"And if it's not?"

Kevin smiles, nears me. "Then we'll deal with it. Together. Okay?"

I nod. But once again I can't seem to move, even though I press down on the mattress with my hands to hoist myself up. Oh, why bother? "Would you let him in?"

Kevin chuckles. "Sure." He starts to head out of my room.

"Wait! Do I look okay?"

Kevin multitasks by shaking his head and rolling his eyes at the same time. "You're hopeless. This isn't about how you look, stud."

"Oh," I laugh nervously. "It's always about how you look."

"It's always about how *you* look." He turns and heads toward the front door. The buzzer bleats a second time, ratcheting up my queasiness. I glance at the clock on my stack-of-books nightstand. It's only ten after seven. Marc's early, but that's just like him. Kevin stops for a moment and tosses over his shoulder, "You look amazing, by the way. Handsome. In fact, no man at no point in time in the history of the universe has ever looked better."

The buzzer sounds a third time. He hurries away.

I glance at myself in the cheap Fred Meyer mirror hanging from the back of the door. I'm wearing a pair of my oldest jeans, faded, ripped at the knees, paired with a Huskies sweatshirt, also faded, with the sleeves cut off. My feet are bare. "You're exaggerating!" I call after him. Then I whisper, "But only a little." In spite of the lack of refinement, I do look pretty good, if I do say so myself.

I let out a shaky breath and try to laugh as I hear Kevin open our front door and then, distantly, the squeak of the main entrance to the building. Muffled voices.

I imagine I'm being pushed onstage by unseen hands. Pushed onstage to perform in a play I don't know any of the lines to.

"That's life, Jimmy. We make it up as we go along. Just listen to your heart."

I swear the voice comes from out of nowhere. I close my eyes for a second, and an image of Miriam rises up. God, I loved that woman. She was my savior. *Is* my savior, my angel.

The voices come closer, and before I have the chance to even think that one of the voices does *not* sound like Marc, they're both standing in the entrance to my bedroom, peering in at me.

I want to do one of those double takes people do in the movies—close my eyes, shake my head to clear it, then look again.

It's not Marc.

"This guy says he knows you." Kevin stands just behind Frasier, the guy I met only yesterday. The tweaker, I called him before I knew his name. And right now, he's obviously tweaking. He can't stand still. I can see from here he's grinding his teeth, and even though our apartment is cool, probably no warmer than sixty-eight degrees, he wears a light sheen of sweat on his face.

Over Frasier's head, Kevin's glaring at me. Like me, he knows a tweaker when he sees one, and he's taking this all wrong. I subtly shake my head at Kevin, then look back to Frasier, who grins and says, "I hope this isn't a bad time."

I let out the breath I've been holding since he appeared in my bedroom doorway. I bite my lower lip because I want to say, "Buddy, you couldn't have picked a worse time if you tried." But I check myself with a quick reminder that I gave this kid my number and, yes, even my fuckin' address so I could help him if he needed it.

I just didn't think he'd need help so soon. Or that he would just show up on my doorstep, minutes before a crucial meeting with someone I just might be falling in love with, to my detriment, maybe.

My look to Kevin is a plea for understanding, which must have sunk in because he turns to leave Frasier and me alone. I hear the not-so-subtle closing of Kevin's bedroom door, his TV starting up. Now I'm not so sure what he's thinking. I suppose I have to give him some slack. I wouldn't know what to think either. Except I do.

In fact, if this kid had shown up for Kevin, my first thought would have been *Kev's about to score.*

"Can I come in?" Frasier sounds agitated. In fact, every word out of his mouth has sounded agitated. He takes a step into my bedroom.

I shake my head. "Bro, don't think you and me in the bedroom is a good idea. Not in your current state. Plus." I take a breath and wait for a second because I want what I have to say next to really sink in. "Plus, I have company comin' any minute now."

"Oh, sorry, man. I'll leave."

"No, no." I guide him by his shoulder to the living room. His hair's greasy, and I wonder when was the last time he washed it. An odor wafts off him, like BO but worse. There's a chemical note, harsh, underneath it all. I know the smell   crystal seeping out of the pores.

We go to the living room and sit, him on the couch and me on the beanbag in the corner. He gets up again immediately and starts pacing the room. No surprises there.

"You're using again. Already? *Seriously?*"

He holds up his hand and grins sheepishly. "C'mon, man. I had to finish up my stash, right?"

I shake my head. "Really, dude? You gonna try to pull that shit with me? I threw your stash away yesterday." I visualize flinging the pipe and the pink glassine bag over the railing at Kerry Park. "You're not being cool. And I can't ever help you if you're gonna be dishonest with me."

He comes close, and I can see already the pleading in his eyes. I could script out this little scene, because I've been here so many times myself I know exactly how it could go. I push him away. "You stink."

"Sorry." He drops onto the couch.

I visualize Marc coming up the front steps. What will he think if he sees me here with this other guy? Will Marc know enough to recognize a tweaker? Will it make any difference if he does?

Of course it will make a difference! I answer myself in a booming voice in my head. I do a little side glance at the DVR on the stand under our TV and see it's twenty past seven. I let out an annoyed chuff of breath and then smile at Frasier to minimize it.

"Look, Frasier. I'm glad you came to me. But I don't know what I can do for you right now. Not in the state you're in."

"What state's that? Idaho?" he asks and grins.

I lean in close. "You're fucked up. Let's not play games. Do you want to do it again?" I hold out my hand.

"Do what?"

"Give me what you have." I hold my outstretched palm closer.

"I might as well finish it," he mumbles.

"Oh yeah? So why did you bother even coming here?" I ask. I continue to hold my hand out.

"Thought you might want a hit." He brings out a pipe. A new one, this one looks cleaner and has a longer stem.

I stare at the pipe for a long time, then at him for a long time. "I do. I want a hit." I glance over my shoulder at Kevin's closed door. "I'd be lying if I told you different."

Frasier pulls out a clear glassine bag. It's full of white powder, shards. It makes my mouth water. I snatch it from his hand.

Frasier smiles. And I get it. I get his smile. There's a certain pleasure in being the corruptor, the seducer. There's a certain joy in dragging others down into the slime and muck with you.

"Go ahead, man. Smoke up." He smiles wider.

"Why are you doing this?"

He shrugs. "You seem like a cool guy. And nobody likes to party alone."

I stand up. My hands tremble a bit with need. My stomach hurts, feeling as though it's twisting in on itself. My heart beats hard in my chest, faster and faster, so fast it scares me. Already I'm thinking about grabbing Frasier and slipping out the back door, what excuse I can make up to give Kevin and, eventually, to Marc.

Am I gonna do this?

No. No, of course not. I hurry into the bathroom between Kevin and my rooms. Frasier follows. "What the fuck?"

I don't give him a chance to stop me. I don't give *myself* a chance to stop me. I pull up the resealable closure on the tiny baggie and upend it over the toilet. The drug falls into the water, the bigger pieces freefalling to the bottom of the bowl. I push a shard that clings to the side off into the water with my foot. And then I flush, holding the empty bag up in a kind of triumph.

"Dude. That shit cost me over a hundred and forty bucks! You owe me."

I move close to Frasier. "No. You owe me. You try this again, and you'll get the same result." Sweat has broken out on my forehead. I'm not so much in shock that I did it to this guy I hardly know, but more in disbelief that I did it to myself. I know I wanted that stuff—bad. I guess the urge never goes away.

And that's a sobering thought.

Frasier's slack-jawed. "You didn't think I was serious, did you?" I ask him.

"I think you're nuts." He looks longingly at the toilet.

While he's looking, I snatch the pipe from his hand. Quickly, I wrap it in toilet paper, and then, in the sink, I smash it. I smile at him again.

Frasier says nothing for a minute or two. He shrugs. "I can just get another one. They're five bucks at a smoke shop on Broadway."

I nod. "That's your choice." I turn and go back into the living room. It's seven thirty now, and I think, with a little nervous tremor, that Marc will be here any minute. I don't want Frasier here when Marc arrives. I can't have him here. One, Marc could get the wrong idea, and believe me, there are *lots* of wrong ideas he could get. And two, I need to be alone with Marc. I need to have that space and that intimacy of one-on-one to say what I need to say to him.

In the living room, I sit on the couch, dying for a cigarette, but it will have to wait. Frasier moves to sit too. I hold up a hand. "Don't. You're going."

"You really want me to go? Go buy a pipe? Some more T?" But he doesn't sit. He doesn't leave either. I can see what looks like despair on his face, or maybe it's confusion. He didn't come here to get high with me.

He came because he was lost.

"That's not what you're gonna do. You didn't show up on my doorstep because you wanted to party with me. You came here because you needed me to stop you." I smile. "Because, right now, you can't stop yourself."

Frasier looks hurt, but I see a little relief mixed in with the pain, the way a patch of blue can peek through a sky clogged with gray clouds. I give him what I hope is a kind smile and not one of victory. "Mission accomplished." I hold up my empty hands. "I stopped you."

Frasier backs against the wall, the one closest to our front door, his hands clutched behind his back. Even though I guess the kid can be no more than his early twenties, he looks older. Pasty skin, dark circles under green eyes. When did he last sleep? I can see him swallowing. I'm about to offer water when he says, voice pitched just above a whisper, "Thanks."

Someone is thanking *me* for stopping him from using? This is truly a new chapter. I stand, and I turn him toward the front door. "You're welcome. You're always welcome. The single most important thing I can tell you right now is this. I. Am. Here. For. You."

He nods. "What am I gonna do now?"

I laugh. "Change of plans from what you thought you had laid out for your Saturday night, huh?"

"I don't know what I expected."

"You came here," I say.

"Exactly. But I repeat. What am I gonna do now?"

I press a hand to my forehead. "I have the feeling you expect me to say you can crash here or something. Especially when I just flushed your stash and broke your pipe. But I can't let you do that for two reasons. One, my roomie, Kevin, would not allow it."

Something occurs to me—a little epiphany. "He's to me what I am to you now." Frasier's eyebrows come together in confusion. I tell him, "Don't worry. That'll make sense later. I hope." I breathe in and then out, almost a little sigh. "And two, someone very important to me is coming by any minute now."

And as soon as the words are out of my mouth, as if fate ordained it, the buzzer sounds.

"Ah! I think he's here. And he and I need to have an important conversation. Alone." I point toward the kitchen. "There's a back door. I need you to leave that way. Now. No argument. I don't know what you'll do with the rest of your night, but I'm trusting you no longer have the funds or the will to use again." An idea comes to me, one I should have had sooner. "Listen. There's an NA meeting in about an hour at the LGBT center on Cap Hill. Go. Now you have something to do." I smile.

He gives me a sheepish grin that allows him to have some of his youth back. In fact, he looks like a little boy. "I might as well. I don't really have any place else to go."

And *that* gets my heart. It's cold out there. It's probably raining.

The buzzer sounds again.

I shut my eyes, feeling just as I did a short time ago, paralyzed.

Chapter Sixteen

MARC

I'm not sure what I expect to feel as I watch Jimmy come to the front door in his bare feet. He's smiling. Any fool could read that smile—he's delighted to see me. I could look at that smile and easily pretend everything's normal.

It's tempting, save for the fact that things couldn't possibly be further from normal.

In spite of myself, I grin back.

I didn't expect to be happy to see him. If you'd asked me, as I walked to this very front door in the rain, in the dark of night, for my prediction on what I'd feel, I would have guessed rage. I would have laid odds on it.

Yeah, anger. Rage.

So why the hell am I giving him a smile?

He opens the door. He looks young. Fresh. Handsome. Dare I say it? Wholesome.

"I'm so glad you came." He opens the door for me, steps back to let me inside. He jumps in front of me to lead me to his own front door, and damned if I don't take a quick glance at his ass as it rises and falls on his trip up the short flight of stairs leading to his apartment. I shake my head at my body's own perfidy, its will-of-its-own reaction to a fine-looking young man.

That's what Jimmy is. I can't deny it. Even back when we first met, as twisted and horrible as that night was, I still remember opening the door to him. Looking back at that moment, it was like Dorothy opening the door to Munchkinland. Suddenly the world was in color. I was thrilled. He was cuter than the pics he'd posted online. Much cuter. I thought I'd made a good choice inviting this rough-around-the-edges guy into my home. It didn't take long to prove myself wrong! Here in this moment, that last thought causes a little twinge to rise up inside, a little flicker of nausea.

He's standing at his front door now, waiting for me to precede him into the apartment. Still smiling. Hope radiating out of that fresh-scrubbed face like a beacon. He looks way better than he did that night two years ago. Younger. Healthier. Full of vitality.

A selfish part of me wants to tell him to forget about resolving things. Let's just hop into bed, get that frat boy getup off you, and get down to business.

But I won't be that stupid. Not again.

I go into the apartment. I refuse now to smile back. I even give him what I know is my best wary and disapproving glance.

There's a weird sense to the living room—a kind of energy I can't put my finger on. It's like something just happened here. Who knows what? Reality tells a different story. It's just a run-down and empty living room, save for us. There's dust on every surface. A stack of paperback novels on top of the TV stand, which is made from cheap particleboard crafted to look like wood. The rug, a Persian knockoff, turns up at one corner where a Converse sneaker lies, like a dead body, on its side. The coffee table is littered with an old issue of *Time*, a bunch of remotes, and a small plate with crumbs on it. Above the nonworking fireplace is a mirror, gilt-edged, with a little mottling on its silvered surface.

I catch sight of myself and think how I look like death. I dressed, with no conscious thought, all in black for our encounter. My hair's still damp and darker from the rain coming down hard outside. And my face? It looks petrified. Like what I want to do more than anything else is turn and run.

And maybe I do.

But I need to see this through. Whatever the outcome will be. We both, I think, need some kind of resolution to move on, wherever that moving on takes us.

I drop onto the couch, legs spread before me. I kick off my shoes, trying to strike a casual pose, as though to say *If anyone should be nervous here, it's not me. It's you, Jimmy.* After all, I did nothing wrong.

Did I?

I force that niggling little question back into my subconscious.

Jimmy stands in front of me, wringing his hands. "Glad you're here, Marc." He swallows. His gaze darts around the room and finally lights on me once more. He's still smiling, but now the expression has morphed into one of sick fear. "You want somethin'? You hungry? A drink?" He glances toward the kitchen. "I got some Coke." He chuckles nervously. "Cola, I mean. I know you like it."

I shake my head. "I don't need anything." I sigh. "Can we just get this over with?"

As soon as the words are out of my mouth, however much I can justify them as deserved, I feel bad because Jimmy looks crestfallen. I never really realized what that word meant before this moment. His smile, the very light of him, is snuffed out by my harshness. It makes me feel both guilty and powerful, all at the same time.

He sits near, but not next to me on the couch. He's clutching his hands together, wringing them. "I guess I deserve that," he says softly.

And then I feel what I predicted. The rage comes upon me all of a sudden, like a horde of bees buzzing around inside my brain. I feel the heat of my face flush. I want to hit him, which is a totally foreign sensation. I don't think I've ever laid hands on another person in anger in my whole life.

And I won't now. But it startles me that the urge rises up, undeniable, that I possess the capacity.

Jimmy begins to talk. "I want to thank you for coming over. I know you didn't have to. I know you probably didn't want to. So I get that you're doing me a favor. A big one." He leans toward me.

I hold up my hand. "Shut up."

He leans back, and his shoulders rise up to meet his neck, as if I really did hit him. His mouth drops open.

"I said shut up. Shut. The. Fuck. Up. Got it?"

He nods, and his eyes are alive with what I see as terror. He folds his arms across his chest. Is it a protective gesture?

"You might think I came here to hear your side of things. Why you did what you did to me. But you flatter yourself, Jimmy. Or is it JD tonight?" I shake my head. "But *I* need to speak. *I* need for you to know just what you did. Just how you hurt me." I stop, a little breathless. That urge to pummel him is mixed now with a sudden need that I fight with all my will—to cry. I won't give in to it. I won't allow him to see my pain, not to that extent.

I go on. "Listen, what you did was terrible. It wasn't so much that you stole from me. Except for two precious items, everything you took could be and probably was replaced. But those two things? One was my grandpa's ring. He left that to me, man. It wasn't worth a whole lot, as I guess you found out when you pawned it, but it was a piece of *him*, and I really loved my grandpa. I lost him too soon…" My words trail off. I'm struggling mightily now not to cry. I draw in a big quivering breath. I clench and unclench my fists. I think of that ring, my mom handing it to me when I came home from college for Grandpa's funeral after his sudden heart attack. He was her father, and she clutched the ring in her hand, eyes rimmed in red, waiting for me. All she wanted in that moment was to give it to me, knowing she was passing along a little bit of his legacy.

My only comfort is that I'll always have that memory, but not the ring. I guess the memory is what counts? Scant comfort…

"You don't have the ring, do you?" A flame of hope flickers to life inside me, hopeless as I know it is.

He shakes his head, staring at me like a dog waiting to be hit.

And for just a moment, I hate him. And I think how I never hated anyone, not really, in my whole life.

I lean back into the couch cushions, my mind awash with disjointed thoughts. I can't remember what I wanted to say. I only know that I want to hoist myself up off this couch and get out of here. I contemplate doing just that when Jimmy says, his voice a sad whisper, "You said two things."

"What?"

"You said you lost two things that night. I need to hear what the second thing was. Please."

I close my eyes. The hatred I felt just a minute ago diminishes just a tiny bit. And maybe an even tinier bit of respect for the man rises up. "Okay. The other thing? The other thing was you took something from me that I don't know how to explain. I had you into my house, man! I trusted you. It never crossed my mind that someone I'd have over, someone I'd be intimate with, would steal from me. Believe it or not, I never had a hookup do that to me ever." I smile bitterly. "And I've had more than a few hookups." I look down at the floor, thinking of the number of hookups I've had, especially back when I first met Jimmy. That number is impossible to quantify, I'm embarrassed to think.

I steer myself away from such musings and continue my diatribe. "The things you took were just things, even that damned ring, but you took something from me that went a lot deeper." I stop and take a breath. "You took my trust. Not just in you, but in people. You stole my judgment, which I was naïve enough to think was pretty good. Now I doubt myself so much that it's hard for me to let anyone else in." I stop and catch my breath. That last realization just came to me in the heat of this moment, and it grips me like icy fingers with its raw truth.

Is Jimmy—or JD—the reason I haven't been able to get close to *anyone* in the recent past? Did he spoil me? And not in a good way?

"I'm sorry," Jimmy says softly.

"No. No, I'm not ready for your apology. I don't know that I'm even finished here." I stare at him. And something occurs to me—he's just another guy, another human being, crafted of the same stuff as I am. Again, I'm overcome by a paradox: wanting to wrap my fingers around his throat and wanting to wrap my arms around him. The way my feelings pull against each other, so contrary, is almost overwhelming. I honestly feel like entertaining both ideas is a portal to insanity. I can't maintain both for long.

So which do I choose? I have no fucking idea.

"Do you get it?"

He nods. "I think I do. And I'm ashamed."

"You took a piece of *me* that night. It's a piece I don't know that I can ever replace. So while you might see that night as a little bit of ripping some gullible dude off, I see it as something much bigger."

"I don't see it that way," he says, and I think too quickly.

"Are you sure?" I ask.

"What do you mean?"

"I just wonder about your empathy," I say. And all of a sudden, I feel like I'm beating a dead horse.

"You shouldn't," he says. "You shouldn't wonder. I get what you went through, what you still go through, and it hurts me, too, more than you know. I don't say that to try to make you feel sorry for me, but because it's true. Back in those days, I did lots of things I'm not proud of. Some of them make me shudder, make me feel sick to think about. Sometimes I can give myself a little relief by looking at that time as though I was another person.

"And I was. A different person. That's what I want you to know, Marc. I'm not that guy who ripped you off. I'm not that addict. Well, I am, but my recovery means more to me than getting high these days. But the drug, where I was then, *who* I was then, all contributed to me being able to do things I can't even imagine doing now.

"I hurt you. And I understand how. Maybe I'll never understand why. And that's kind of okay. But I need you to know, with all my heart, that it *wasn't personal*. Not only the T, although that was a big factor, but everything in my life that brought me to that point in your place two years ago, all those things played a part in me being somebody I no longer am."

"That's easy to say," I challenge, but already I feel my rage subsiding and my understanding growing, as much as I don't want it to. I want him to suffer more, but what's the point in that?

"It's not so easy, Marc. It's not easy to admit my mistakes, the hard stumbles I made on my journey, especially when they hurt someone as innocent and undeserving as you. But I grew from those fuckups. I learned how to be a better person." He pauses for a moment. "So the one thing I *won't* say to you is that I regret what I did. I'm so, so sorry that you got hurt, of course, but I don't regret any steps I've taken on my journey. I can't. *All* those steps, not just the ones I'm proud of, make me the guy you see sitting here before you tonight.

"And that guy is decent. And that guy deserves a second chance. And that guy deserves love."

Jimmy stares down at the floor, his shoulders moving up and down almost imperceptibly. Still staring at the floor, what he says next is marked by sadness. "Even if it doesn't come from you."

It's almost too much to process. I stand and walk to the window. I look out at the rain-smeared street scene before me, the way the streetlamps reflect on the slick black pavement. The long columns of reflected light stretch out on the street. I think if I look at them just right, they're like pillars of light rising up.

I look back at Jimmy on the couch. He's lifted his head, and his face is free of tears. Yet he stares off into the distance as though he's elsewhere.

At last he notices me looking and gives me a tentative smile. "What?"

I shake my head. "Just you."

"What about me?"

I want to tell him he's horrible, a user and a thief. But even I don't believe it. Not anymore. Oh, I know it will take a while for that realization to get really deep down inside, in my heart, where it matters, but at least there's a glimmer of something there. Something my heart can see as truth.

Jimmy leans forward. "Look. If you want to walk out that door, I won't try to stop you. I can't control you or control what you think. I can only be who I am. And that person, tonight, cares about you, Marc. And wants to know if we can get past..." he trails off.

One of the bedroom doors creaks open. I look up to see a disheveled young man peering out at us.

I look to Jimmy. "Your roommate?"

Jimmy shakes his head. "No. Just a friend. I told him he could crash here tonight. He's in trouble. Aren't you, Frasier?"

The guy looks from me to Jimmy, back to Jimmy again. He shrugs.

Jimmy stands. "Frasier here is a tweaker. Like I used to be. Like I always will be, I guess. I need to help him. Is that okay with you?"

I don't know what to think. I thought I had a small handle on Jimmy's world, but that handle just got slippery and my hand tore loose. "Sure," I say softly. "Whatever." I turn to the door. "I'm gonna go. Okay?"

Jimmy's face looks sad. "I said I wouldn't stop you. But Marc, know this. In order to continue my recovery and stay on the sober line, I know I need to reach out to other people, give them what some people were generous enough to give to me. It's time."

There's nothing in me left to say. Stomach churning, I turn and head for the door, longing for rain and the dark, dark night. Just as I pull it open, Jimmy calls after me, "And maybe I don't just mean my tweaker friend here."

*

Jimmy's words ring in my ears like an echo as I step out into the night. The rain has stopped, and the sky's cleared. I can even see a few stars. The moon's high and almost full. A wind off the Sound brings the smell of saltwater.

What did Jimmy mean by that last remark? Was he talking about me? Even as I start up the street, away from his apartment building, I chastise myself. Who am I trying to kid? Of course he was.

Pardon the pun, but it's a sobering thought. My promiscuity and recklessness in the past—as exemplified by inviting a crystal meth addict who robbed me blind into my home—have been something I've glossed over, afraid to look it in the eye, for fear of seeing myself reflected back.

They say it takes one to know one. Does Jimmy see another addict when he looks at me?

No, it's not possible. I like sex, but I'm not an addict, for Christ's sakes. If we consider hooking up and cruising online as an addiction, most younger, and many older, gay men need a twelve-step group, right?

Right.

Of course. I continue on my way to the bus stop a block away, trying to think of anything but Jimmy. Of anything but this night. And how something went wrong—yet I still am having trouble putting my finger on just *what*.

What do I have recorded on the old DVR at home? Maybe an hour of *Grey's Anatomy*, and a few tears shed will help keep the mind free of more pressing concerns.

Sure.

Right now, for example, I notice that the clearing sky combined with the dampness has caused the temperature to plunge. I wouldn't be surprised if it's now close to, or at, freezing. I pull the collar of my jacket up close to my chin and give a little shiver.

And then I spy him, standing on the corner, under a streetlamp. He makes me pause.

The illumination endows him with an almost otherworldly glow, like he's an angel.

As I get closer, I determine that he's certainly cute enough to be an angel. In spite of all the trauma tonight, a little smile curls up the corners of my lips.

Curly blond hair, a small compact body, jeans, running shoes, and a dark-colored fleece. His breath steams out, little clouds.

I start to pass by, thinking he's nothing more than a handsome stranger, a ship I pass in the night, but then he stops me. He reaches out and touches my shoulder.

"Hey," he says.

I start to smile, turn on the charm. Make eye contact. But when I look at his face, I see he's not the wholesome kid I thought he was. The mop of curly blond hair, his diminutive height and slight frame, gave him the appearance of someone much younger. Now, looking closer at his grin, I can see he might be as old as I am, late thirties, early forties. His nose is a little crooked, as if it might have once been broken. There's a chip off one of his front teeth. The skin around his eyes sags a bit, just like I notice my own have begun to do. A scar separates one of his eyebrows.

He pulls out a cigarette and puts it in his mouth. It bobs up and down as he asks, "Got a light?"

I shake my head and make to move on.

He reaches out and grabs my shoulder—again. Hard. It stops me. When I look back at him, a little stunned, he grins. He gropes around in his pocket and pulls out a disposable lighter. The flare of its flame illuminates his face even more, giving it an almost demonic appearance.

My heartbeat quickens.

He exhales twin plumes of smoke through his nostrils, takes another drag, and blows the second stream of smoke toward my face. I want to wave it away, but I resist.

"Sorry. Guess I had a lighter after all."

Now I wish he'd smile, but he simply stares at me with eyes that seem dead, flat. It's like he's sizing me up.

"What are you doing out on this rainy night?" he asks.

I swallow, or at least try to. My mouth is suddenly dry. I cut my gaze left, then right. There's no one around. The street is eerily quiet—and deserted. I wonder how late it is. Could I have been at Jimmy's for *that* long? I mean, it can't be much later than ten, at the latest.

And yet, here's me and this guy.

All alone.

"I, uh, gotta be getting home," I tell him and try to move away.

But his hand, still on my shoulder, holds fast. His fingers dig painfully into my shoulder, and I start to get scared.

"What's your hurry?" He looks me up and down in an appraising sort of way, and I think I might have once warmed to his gaze, thinking how he's checking me out. And yes, he *is* checking me out. There's no doubt about that. But I'm not sure *what* he's appraising me for. And that chills me.

"I gotta get home. Feed my cat." My voice is higher-pitched, and I curse myself. I sound silly. And scared.

He chuckles, takes another drag. "You like to party?"

"What?"

"You know. Don't try to pretend you're all innocent and shit. Party. Get high." He wiggles his eyebrows. "Get high and fuck around?"

I yank myself away. His hand at last slips from my shoulder. "I don't party, and like I said, I need to get home."

A car goes by, its tires hissing on the wet pavement. I turn to peer desperately at the driver, but all I can see is a ghostly face, pale in the darkness. My fight-or-flee instinct has risen up, like the hairs on my neck. And for me, fleeing is always the best option. I want to turn and run, fast as I can, down the street. Hell, I want to run out in front of that car, waving my arms and pleading for help.

But I'm a civilized guy, right? I can't do either, not without the fear of looking like a crazy person. And right now, that fear is greater than the fear I have for this guy, despite the red flags of alarm he's causing to rise inside me.

He smiles, and I don't think I've ever seen something as chilling as that smile. It's completely devoid of warmth, the antithesis, really, of a smile.

It's menacing.

"C'mon, Mary," he says. "I see queens like you cruising around all the time. I know what you're looking for." He leans in close and whispers. "I'm holding."

I gulp. "Holding what?"

"My dick, you knucklehead." He snorts. "Tina, of course. You want a taste? We can smoke up right back in that alley." He nods to the alley behind him. Its dark opening looks like a maw to me. There's no way I'd go back there with him.

And all at once, I think of a summer night on Capitol Hill, when I did pretty much just that. Found a cute guy, this one dark with a buzz cut and a beard. We were both out ambling around after the bars had closed. And with only the language of a few flirtatious gazes, I slipped into an alley with him and sucked him off.

The opening to that alley didn't look all that different from the one before me right now. I shake my head. "I can't, man."

Softly, he reaches in the pocket of his fleece. He pulls out a switchblade, holds it covertly to his side. He clicks it open, and the blade glints off the yellow of the streetlamp. "My friend here begs to differ."

My knees turn to water, but I'm able to manage standing anyway.

"Let's go, Mary."

He presses the knife to my back, directing me with it into the alley. I feel myself going numb, as if the world is vanishing around me. I can't think of what to do, other than comply.

We get back a way, near a dumpster that smells of rotting vegetables and old grease. He turns to me, makes to unzip. When he sees me looking down, he bursts into laughter. He takes his hand off his fly.

"I need your wallet. Your watch too." He lifts the edge of my jacket arm to see if I'm wearing one. "Nice," he says.

I begin to shake. I hand him what he asks for and wonder if this is all he'll take.

I should have stayed with Jimmy. The thought appears, then vanishes.

"We good?" I ask.

He looks me up and down.

And then he raises the knife.

Chapter Seventeen

JIMMY

"Was that somebody special?" Frasier asks.

We're standing like players on a stage, frozen in the middle of my living room. The slam of the door after Marc's exit seems to echo, but I know I'm imagining that. Just me being me—melodramatic. Still, I stare at the door for long seconds, hoping it will magically open again, and Marc will come back.

He doesn't.

And the creak and slam of the vestibule door confirms his exit. I doubt that he'll ever return. And I begin to think this is one I might need to chalk up to experience, to simply move on. What was so special about Marc anyway? I shake my head, thinking I need to make a list. A long list.

I turn back to Frasier, sighing. "Yeah. He was somebody special. Was." I smile, but there's no joy in it, only a sense of deep resignation and sadness.

"Sorry. I hope I didn't screw things up."

"What the hell made you come out of my room, anyway?" I snap and then immediately regret it. The poor guy has done nothing wrong. Not when he's here at my invitation. I attempt a smile. "Sorry. You didn't screw anything up. I think I did that already. What's that term?"

Frasier's eyebrows come together, reflecting his confusion. He shrugs and then shakes his head.

The word comes to me. "Fubar. Fucked up beyond all repair." I laugh hard, but Frasier doesn't join me. When I rein it in, he stares at me like I'm some sort of lunatic.

And maybe I am. "Did you need something?" I ask finally.

"I'm not gonna be able to sleep tonight," he says flatly. "Not in my fucked-up state."

I plop down on the couch, put my head in my hands, try to breathe in and out slowly, as I know I'm supposed to do when I'm stressed.

"And this is my problem how?" I finally ask.

"It's not. I just wondered if maybe…" It's my turn to fill in the blank.

"If maybe I had something to help you sleep?" I raise my eyebrows, lift my head, and turn toward him. "Dude, I'm an addict. I don't even keep beer in the house." I lay my head on the back of the couch, thinking. "In the medicine cabinet, there's some Nyquil from the last time I had a cold. That might help."

"Yeah," Frasier chuckles. "Like taking aspirin for a broken arm."

I shrug. "Best I can do."

He shuffles off to the bathroom. He'll probably down the remainder of the Nyquil in a couple of swallows. Who knows? Maybe it will calm him down. Not enough to sleep, that's for sure, but maybe enough to lie still and rest until dawn creeps into my bedroom.

I hear him flush the toilet, then go from the bathroom to the bedroom. The door closes. In his bedroom, Kevin's TV is going. A laugh track explodes, making me feel even more out of it, more alone.

And I suddenly feel out of place in my own home. What am I going to do?

Should I chase after him?

It's too late. Too much time has passed. He's probably already on a bus, headed home, cursing that he gave me the small amount of time he did. What was it worth, anyway? Who did it help?

If only he would have let me explain more...

I won't let myself go back and regret what I said or didn't say. All I could do was ask for forgiveness. If he can't let it go, then I really must. I need to forgive myself.

I stand up, pace the room. I glance over at the couch, thinking that will be my bed tonight. It's okay. I'm helping a fellow traveler on this fucked-up journey. And that's a good thing. Yay me.

Yet I feel restless, as though I haven't done enough.

I glance over at the mirror on the wall. Its mottled surface reflects my anguish back. I don't think I realized how upset I was until I had a glimpse of my own face. I look stricken. Is that the right word?

Just as I turn my gaze away from the mirror, there's a glimmer of movement over my shoulder. I look back at the mirror, and of course, there's nothing there.

But there *was* something there. I swear it. It was like someone moved, over by the front door. I shut my eyes.

And I see her. Miriam. It's just like she's standing by the front door, nodding her head back toward it, trying to tell me something.

I scratch my head, wondering if I did the wrong thing by throwing out Frasier's party favors. Maybe a little oblivion, tonight, is just what I need. And I was too stupid and/or blind to see it.

No. That's never the answer, a little voice says in my head. A voice that doesn't sound like my own.

I know Miriam's right. She always is.

And I think I know what the little nod of her head means, whether I'm imagining it or not.

"Go," she's saying. "Go out and find him. Now is not the time for a text or a phone call."

And this time, the little voice I hear morphs from Miriam's to my own.

And I make sense.

I go get my jacket. Put it on. Sit down on the couch to slip into my sneaks.

I stand. If I have to walk all the way to Marc's place, I will. But tonight we'll make things right—or at least as right as they can be.

I can only do my best.

I pause outside both bedroom doors and say, loudly, "I'm going out. Don't know when I'll be back, but I've got my phone."

There's no response from behind either door. That's what I figured. And I'm relieved. I head out.

*

When the frigid cold's seeping into my clothes, and I appear to be the only soul on the streets, I hear the muffled sob.

I stop, listening. A ferry on Puget Sound blasts a horn into the night. I want to shush it.

I hear a short hiccup of breath.

I look all around me. I'm almost home. In fact, the idea of stretching out on the couch with a blanket over me has started to sound very tempting. I can almost imagine the warmth and the comfort.

There's another intake of trembling breath. Someone somewhere is crying.

I look up and down the street. Farther south, a pickup truck grumbles just before making a left turn. A bag lady, in that same direction, totters into view. It's too dark to see any distinguishing features, but I can hear the wobble of one crooked wheel on the shopping cart she's pushing, which is piled high with her stuff.

But she's too far away for me to hear her sobbing.

I slow, and then I spy the opening to the alley, about six or so feet ahead of me. Right in front of my eyes, in fact.

I rub my head, thinking of simply ignoring the sound. Belltown, my neighborhood, is a curious mix of the rich and the poor. Amazon and Microsoft executives and homeless heroin addicts mingle on its streets. The litter in the gutter contains everything from PBR cans, tiny glassine bags, and syringes to Starbucks cups and ticket stubs from the Moore Theatre.

That sound? It could be a ploy. Probably *is* a ploy to entice me into the alley. I know; I've been the one setting a trap. Because of its mix of the desperate and the overfed, Belltown is an area ripe for crime, for setting traps for the unwary, for the bleeding heart wanting only to help.

I approach the alley warily, thinking I can dash away if need be.

It takes a couple of minutes even for my dark-adapted eyes to adjust to the shadows in the alley.

But when they do adjust, I see a form huddled near the dumpster. Knees curled up, almost fetal position. It's too dark to tell much more about this person crying on the filthy and cold ground.

I move closer.

He looks up.

And for a moment the wind rushes out of me. For a moment I'm not sure I can believe my eyes.

It's Marc.

I rush over to him, kneel beside him. I peer into his face, his wild, wet, and red-rimmed eyes. I do a quick scan, as best I can, of the rest of him. He appears to be okay—physically, at least. There's no blood, no obvious signs of trauma, save for his dirty clothes, his ripped jacket, his shivering.

"Hey, what happened? Are you okay?"

He looks up at me, confused, like I fell out of the sky.

"How did you know I was here?"

"I didn't. I just, I just…" my voice trails off. I have an odd feeling, one I don't want to trust but one I can't deny. I did know he was there. I did know he needed help. I don't know how. I don't know why.

But why are those questions even important? If there's one thing I've learned in being sober, it's that we have inexplicable feelings about stuff, and those feelings are seldom wrong.

"What difference does that make?" I gather him up in my arms and hold him, right here on the bricked surface of the alley, heedless of the cold, the damp, and the grit.

Marc clings to me. "I guess it doesn't. I'm just glad you found me," he mumbles into my shoulder. I squeeze him harder.

We're like that for a while, just two men clinging to one another the way a drowning man might hang on to something that floats. Except I don't know which of us is the drowning man and just what exactly it is that floats.

Hope?

Again, does it matter? We're here for each other when it counts.

After a while, I ask again, "Are you okay? Can you stand up?"

He gives out a snotty snort of laughter. "Nothing's hurt. Physically, at least. Save for my pride."

"What happened?"

"I was robbed. He had a knife, but he just used it to scare me." He laughs again, and it ends in a spasm of coughs. Or are they sobs? "Boy, he succeeded."

"What did he take?"

"Wallet, watch."

"I'm sorry."

He waves me away. He scoots a bit over so we're no longer connected. "What are you sorry for? *You* robbed me two years ago. And you had the decency to be sneaky about it so I wouldn't be scared while I was getting fleeced." He laughs again. "You're a considerate bandit."

I can't join him—what he says isn't funny. I feel a little sick inside.

"At least you weren't mean about it. At least I forgive you."

It takes a minute for the words to sink in. When they do, I seek out his eyes in the darkness. "You do?"

He nods. "You said it. You're not that same person."

And just like that, my spirit's lifted. There's a lightening, as though a weight I didn't know I was carrying around got removed. I don't want to press. I don't want to ask him to repeat himself, just so I can make sure of what I heard. I'm afraid that if I do, he'll recant. Tell me I heard him wrong.

So I help him to his feet. Brush what grit and dirt I can off him. He's still shaking, and I take him in my arms again, squeeze. "I'm gonna squeeze those shakes right out of you, man."

Marc leans back a little. Smiles.

"What do you wanna do?" I ask. "Want me to call the cops?"

He shakes his head. "Nah. Maybe later. I doubt that there's much they can do."

"You should still file a report."

"Like I said, maybe later." A sob erupts out of him like a hiccup. "I just wanna go home!"

I nod. "Sure. Sure you do."

"Let's go find a cab," he says. "I'm in no state for the bus. Not tonight."

We emerge from the alley. The streetlights seem unnaturally bright. Marc stops, pats his pockets. "Shit."

"What?" I ask, although then the answer comes to me before he even says it.

"No wallet." He shrugs. "Guess we can walk. It's not that far." He shivers.

I pull out my own wallet and look inside. There's a sad single twenty in there. It's all I have until payday next week. I stuff the wallet back in my jeans. "I've got enough for a cab," I tell him, hoping like hell I'm right.

"I'll pay you back."

"Don't you even think about it. It's my treat. I owe you."

He snorts again. I'm not sure if he's laughing or crying. "You certainly do."

We both look as we see a Yellow Cab coming down the street toward us. "Here you go," I say. "You just want some cash? Or you want me to come with you?" I want, more than I've ever wanted anything, for him to say "Come with me," but I would understand if he didn't.

He doesn't say, and we stand at the curb, waiting for the cab to glide up beside us. I look over at Marc.

"Get in the damn cab," he says.

Chapter Eighteen

MARC

The interior of the cab smells damp. Or maybe it's just us. Jimmy sits pressed close to me, heedless of the disapproving stare of the swarthy cab driver in the rearview mirror. I don't care. Let him look. We're paying him to drive us, not judge us. Just to spite him, I lay my head on Jimmy's shoulder and grab one of his hands and intertwine my fingers with his.

I'm still shaking. But the warmth emanating from Jimmy is going a long way to quiet the trembling. I close my eyes.

Darkness. Rough brick walls and the squat shape of a dumpster in the shadows. The guy with the knife rises up before me, terrifying, but then he quickly morphs into Jimmy. I feel my lips curl up in a smile. My heart rate slows. Instead of a knife, Jimmy holds out a big serving spoon. On it, piled high, is a huge scoop of mashed potatoes.

I start to giggle.

Jimmy nudges me. I stir, wondering how I could have fallen asleep so quickly, so completely. "Hey, you. This the right place?"

I feel disoriented, like I slept a lot longer than the few minutes I must have. I look up at the building to our right, and even though logically I know it's home, it doesn't look familiar. It's just a three-story red brick apartment house, rectangular, built in the 1990s. Is it mine? Why isn't it ringing a bell? Do I need to click my heels together or something?

I shake my head. "Yeah, that's it." It's got to be, right? I'm probably in a bit of shock from the mugging. I've heard feeling disoriented is part of the package.

"Course it is, silly."

That's right. Jimmy has been here before.

I sit silently, trying to get my brain in gear as Jimmy pays the driver. He gets his change and opens the door.

I just sit there. There's this feeling of numbness. This mundane scene has all the earmarks of the surreal.

He smiles. "You ready?"

I nod and lean into him. He takes my hand and pulls me from the cab.

"Good night," he leans in to tell the cabbie.

And what the cabbie says surprises me. I had him all wrong. "You two take care. Get him to bed!"

"We will. And I will. Thanks."

Before I know it, we're cutting across the parking lot at the front of the building. "I don't remember which one is yours," Jimmy says.

I laugh. "Neither do I." I lower myself down on one of the little concrete things they have in front to stop parking cars from running into the building. Do they have a name? Should I know it? I laugh again. It would probably be better to remember which apartment is mine. More useful.

Jimmy sits beside me. "Are you kidding?"

"I wish I was." I twist to look up at the building over my shoulder. There's a staircase leading up to a narrow walkway that fronts the upstairs units. That same staircase, at ground level, heads downward to a patio. Yes, okay. A little bit of certainty filters in. I know the building is built into a bluff above a greenbelt. It overlooks Lake Union.

"My apartment's on the second floor." I grope in my pockets for my keys. When my hand doesn't immediately land on them, my heart starts to hammer, acid rises up in my throat, and beads of cold sweat break out on my forehead. *Oh God, did he take my keys too? Is he up there now? Waiting with his damned knife?*

I feel like my legs are turning liquid, and I hold on to Jimmy for support.

"What?"

"He took my keys!" I gasp, just as my fingers close around them. "Sorry." I peer into Jimmy's eyes. I lift the keys out and jingle them. "They're right here."

"Is there an apartment number on them?" He reaches for my key ring, and I let him take it.

"I'm in 202." Just like that, my brain fills in the missing piece. Where it came from, I can't say. But I know it for sure. How weird. Forgetting my own address.

"Let's go." Jimmy takes my hand, giving me a slight tug.

We head up the stairs.

Inside, Jimmy tells me to sit on the couch. He busies himself turning on lights. He finds the remote for the TV and flips it on. *American Horror Story.* He immediately mutes the sound. "Don't look!" he cautions me. "You have cable, right?"

I nod. "I think so."

I watch as he changes the channel. I recognize one of the music channel screens. He un-mutes the sound. Soft new age music filters out of my sound bar. I breathe in, out. The music has what I assume is its desired effect—it calms me.

"Thanks," I say softly.

"No worries." Jimmy heads into the kitchen. "I'm gonna make you some tea. Okay if I rummage around out here?"

I throw my head back on the couch. "Knock yourself out. There's a canister on the counter with a bunch of different kinds. Chamomile, Darjeeling, English breakfast, green, mint." Amazing what your memory chooses to retain.

"You got a request?"

I snort. "Yeah. Don't steal my teakettle."

He comes back out from the kitchen and stands in front of me. He looks so worried and hurt. It's kind of cute.

"I'm kidding," I say. I wonder where the mental energy to joke about something so traumatic came from. "The green tea would be nice. With a little honey, honey." I smile.

He pulls the throw at one end of the couch over me before returning to the kitchen.

*

"Why did you have me over?" Jimmy asks as he tucks me into bed. There's something tender in his face—and caring. It makes me feel all warm. I simply want to snuggle down beneath my quilt with the image of that face imprinted in my head.

Sweet dreams, for sure.

"Hmm?" he urges.

Sleepily, I say, "What? Tonight?" I turn on my side, but I still face him. "You had cab fare."

He pokes me. "Don't be stupid. I'm serious. That night. You weren't my typical hookup. And I have a feeling I wasn't your usual choice from the menu either."

I sit up a little, my head just above the pillows, and look over at him. "Sit down," I say.

He does, and the bed creaks as he settles his weight on it.

"You know you're asking me a very deep question when I'm vulnerable. Is that fair?"

"I don't know about fair. But I want to know what you'd say."

I let my head sink down farther into the two pillows under me. I close my eyes, trying to transport myself back to that night. Why *did* I ask him over? I remember his profile and how rough-edged it was—with all the leather, the piercings. Another detail flashes into my head. In all his pics, he wore mirrored aviator sunglasses, so his eyes couldn't be seen.

A shame, because his blue eyes are amazing, kind of crystalline, paradoxically icy and warm. I open my own eyes to look into them now.

Despite my trying to grasp for an answer to his question, the words come to me effortlessly, as though someone else implanted them in my brain.

Or in my heart.

"I was hoping for a miracle." The words slip out without analysis, and I'm left a little in awe at their truth and yet a little confused by what their full meaning is.

"A miracle?" Jimmy stretches out on the bed beside me, hands clasped behind his head and staring up at the ceiling. "I don't think 'miracle' and me have ever been uttered in the same sentence." He laughs a little, but there's a tinge of sadness to his chuckles.

"I didn't say you were a miracle. I said I was hoping for one."

Jimmy sighs. "Point taken."

I need to expound on this, as much for Jimmy's benefit as for my own. "Back then, I did tons of hooking up. Too much, even the most jaded among us will concede that." I think of Don and what he does and doesn't know. Although I've revealed myself to him as a play-the-field type of guy, I have never gone into the extent I played it and how many positions I assumed.

I'm too ashamed.

"And I think every time I hooked up, I was hoping for a miracle." I close my eyes and feel a rapidly expanding lump in my throat. I swallow hard in a wasted effort to diminish it. "Hoping that some man would come over and save me. Save me from myself." I pause, the wheels turning. "Or make me someone else that I'd see through their eyes."

I stop. I don't want this to turn into a pity party, yet the truth's the truth. "I can still feel that anticipation, in the shower, getting ready, knowing my prince was on his way. But what happened in the fairy tales always worked in reverse for me."

"What do you mean?"

"When I would kiss the prince, they'd always turn into a frog."

I expect Jimmy to laugh, but he doesn't. I turn on my side, snuggling into his warmth. "You should have been the biggest frog of all. But through all this time, through all the men that came after you, I could never quite get you out of my head. I told myself it was because you ripped me off, and there was that, but there was more too." I throw one arm over Jimmy's chest.

"There was this," I squeeze him, holding him. "Remember?"

He nods. "Oh, sure. And I never forgot you because there was no one I was with back then that I wanted to cuddle with, for Christ's sake, but I wanted to with you. And that hit me from out of left field. That penetrated right down into my tweaked-out brain. I hated you and loved you at the same time."

"Why hate?"

"Because you showed me something I didn't believe I could have. Because you made me feel things I didn't want to feel. That made me mad. And it made me want to be with you like no one else I'd ever met. Weird, huh?"

"Not weird," I tell him. "Human." I lean forward and kiss him very lightly on the lips. With my hand, I close his eyes and tenderly kiss each lid. "You're just one of us, buddy. You want someone there for you. You want someone to touch. I think that's all any of us wants." I sigh.

Jimmy picks up on what the sigh is saying. "But?"

"But I don't know. Maybe we both had strange ways of trying to find that someone to touch us."

"Oh, I think we could have lived without all that shit!" Jimmy laughs.

"No, no. Hear me out. Saying tonight that I was hoping for a miracle was kind of a wake-up call—for me. I didn't know until those words tumbled from my lips what I'd been looking for. A miracle?" I make a little snorting sound.

"The miracle wasn't you, Jimmy, although I wish I could say it was. It wasn't any man. It wasn't my first boyfriend or my second. It wasn't the cross-country track coach I had a crush on in high school. It wasn't the dad whose affection I always craved and never got because I could never be good enough—or should I say manly enough—for him.

"No, the miracle I was waiting for was *me*." I touch my chest. "Right here in my heart. To know I could not only love but forgive. And see people in my life as the flawed, broken, and beautiful things they are. Just like *me*."

I go quiet with the feeling I have more to say. I just don't know that I have the words right now to express the emotions. It's like some kind of weird pain has been expressed, and now—freedom.

Jimmy says nothing. He raises up to kiss me. And then he simply peers down at me, stroking my face. A little smile plays about his lips.

I feel warm. At home.

I touch his face, revel in the roughness of his stubble beneath my fingertips. "Should we?" I ask. I raise an eyebrow. His lips look so tempting, so delectable, mere inches away.

He chuckles. "Should we what? Go to sleep?" He nods. "Yeah, I think so. After what you've been through tonight—hell, after what *I've* been through tonight—we both need some rest. And I can't imagine anything better than actually falling asleep next to you." He lays his head back down on the pillow.

"And then?" I ask.

"And then we'll see what the morning brings. We don't need to plan a thing. Let's just be."

"Right here? Right now?" I ask.

"Right here. Right now," he responds, and he wraps himself around me, one leg thrown over mine.

Sunday

Chapter Nineteen

JIMMY

I want to serve him breakfast in bed. And before your mind takes a nosedive into the gutter, I'm not talking about waking him up with a blow job or with slapping his cheek with my hard-on, although both have their appeal. And might come later...

Anyway, I think back to when he came into the diner at the beginning of last week, which seemed so coincidental, so random, but I doubt that it was. I guess our paths were meant to cross again. I smile at the sense of humor he displayed in that breakfast-time encounter, little evidence of which I've seen lately, which I know is my own fault. But that meeting? I think it represented unfinished business.

Unfinished love, maybe.

Oh, you cornball! I roll over gently and ever so silently put my bare feet to the floor. Back when I was a dirty addict, I never would have allowed such notions into my pretty little fucked-up head. And maybe that's *why* I was a dirty addict...and a thief. Those particular ways of being really don't allow much room for love.

And certainly the idea of making a guy breakfast would have never crossed my mind. Maybe *stealing* breakfast, if I'd had any appetite at all for food back then as I sneaked out the door with the cash from his wallet in my pocket.

But today is a new day.

Today is a new me.

That's the beauty I've found in recovery—that every day is a new beginning. We can slip. We can fall. We can even relapse. But each new twenty-four-hour period is a gift filled with hope and promise.

A clean slate, right?

And this morning, *this guy* is grateful for the man in bed next to him and wants to demonstrate his gratitude with a sweet little gesture.

I look over my shoulder at Marc sleeping. His lips are parted, almost raised up in a little smile. His breathing is deep and regular. If I lean in close, I can see his eyeballs moving restlessly back and forth under the lids.

I hope he's having sweet dreams.

I get up, wincing as the box springs below us loudly complain. I cast another look over my shoulder, but Marc doesn't stir. Even his breathing doesn't change.

I think of the little miracle that's just passed—I actually spent the night with a guy and didn't have sex! That's a first. Not that I didn't want to, not that I didn't lie close to him throughout the night, my boner waxing and waning, waxing and waning, until it nearly drove me insane.

I wanted him to rest.

I wanted to put him first, to show him I could be unselfish.

Now, as I gaze down at him, my heart's full. I love the way the sunlight outside manages to filter through the blinds on his windows, landing in slats of yellow gold on his sleeping face. I love how broad his shoulders look against his dark-gray sheets. I love the way one nipple peeks out at the top of the sheet. I long to put my tongue to that nipple, but I don't want to wake him.

I move away before temptation erases my good intentions, and I simply hop back in bed, rudely wake him, and jump his bones.

In the corner of the room, I find the clothes I discarded on the floor last night and get dressed in silence. Once I tense as Marc turns over and away from me. But then he begins to snore, and I relax.

In the cab last night, I noticed a little convenience store just a block or two south of Marc's place. I hope it's open.

I creep from his bedroom, through the living room, and emerge onto the walkway outside Marc's front door.

It's early. I have no idea what time it is, but the sun is up behind me and the sky's brilliant blue. Rare for winter, and I'll take the good weather as an omen, a promise.

Why not?

It must have rained during the night, because the street is slick. The air's relatively warm, so Dexter Avenue has a light mist emerging from its pavement.

I head down the stairs, noting the quiet, at least the quiet of this busy city street. A lone bicyclist puffs his way up the hill, coming from the north. He looks over and spots me and gives a little wave. I smile and wave back and think—another omen.

A couple of cars pass as I head south. In between some of the buildings, I can see the sun rising higher, higher over the Cascade Mountains, tangerine against their almost purple silhouettes.

A guy with gray hair, wearing a quilted black jacket and glasses, emerges from a white stucco building ahead of me. He's being led by a little Boston terrier with a red harness. He stops only feet from their front door as she squats near some shrubbery and does her business. She turns immediately to go back inside, and the guy laughs and tries to tug her in the opposite direction. "Come on. Don't you want to go for a little walk?" But the Boston is adamant, and with a sigh, he gives up and follows her back up red brick stairs to disappear into their glass front doors.

Sometimes you just have to let go and not resist. There's another lesson I've learned in recovery—and now from a Boston terrier.

I'm relieved to see the neon Open sign is illuminated in the window of the little convenience store. God, I hope they have what I'm looking for.

Chapter Twenty

MARC

I roll over and open my eyes, feeling more rested than I have in years. It takes me back to when I was a kid, waking in the summer all on my own, with the sun streaming in. The day was new and full of promise. Yeah, that's how I feel.

Right up until the moment I roll over and discover I'm in bed alone.

Once again.

"Jimmy," I call out softly. Then again, louder, "Jimmy?"

I sit up, thinking how fast disappointment can cloud happiness, how a mood can transform in milliseconds. How darkness can snuff out light in an instant.

I'm about to call out again. Then I think *What's the point? He's gone. You should have known.*

Yet, yet... Last night had been so wonderful. I thought we'd made a real connection. I believed my forgiveness not only of him, but also of myself, changed things, offered us a second chance to be what I thought we were—two guys who just might love each other.

I shake my head, letting out a long and low sigh. Sunlight filters in through my blinds, and instead of taking what hints to be a glorious day as a good sign, something to be grateful for, it makes me feel a little nauseous. The sunshine seems wrong somehow. I want to hear rain hitting violently against my window. I want it to still be so dark I need to lean over and turn on the lamp on my nightstand just so I can see on my way to the bathroom.

I want a lot of things.

I want Jimmy to be here.

I want what I drifted off to sleep last night believing to be true—that we'd crossed a bridge toward togetherness, that we'd come to a real meeting of minds, of hearts, of souls.

I get up from bed, stumbling toward the bathroom with my useless boner leading the way, making the front of my plaid boxers stick out. Will I ever attain an age where I wouldn't wake up with a hard-on, regardless of the situation?

As I head toward the bathroom, I have a view of the rest of the little apartment. I quickly scan the living room and the kitchen area with its breakfast bar and two stools. I'm hoping to find Jimmy lying on the couch with the throw over him, snoring. Or better yet, in the kitchen, trying to figure out how to use my French press.

But, as it always is, my home is empty. I should get a pet. Maybe I'll head over to the animal shelter by Ballard today and see what's on offer. We can comfort each other—two mutts nobody wants!

Oh, quit feeling sorry for yourself, Marc. This Sunday morning is just like all the others—you went to bed with a guy on Saturday night and woke up alone and at loose ends on Sunday morning.

You should be used to the routine.

But I'm not.

My heart aches.

And not just for company, but for specific company. I wander over to the living room window and look out on Dexter. It's empty, save for a neighbor across the street, a middle-aged guy who's stepped out on his balcony for what I guess is his first smoke of the day.

I've seen him before.

I head into the bathroom, take care of business, flush.

As I head out to the kitchen to make coffee, I hate myself because I do a quick scan of the place. iPad still on the coffee table? Check. TV's still here. So are my Diesel sneakers by the front door. I tiptoe back into the bedroom, open the Lucite box on my dresser. Everything—a couple of credit cards I rarely use, a few dollars, a cheap Fossil watch—are all still there.

He didn't steal.

He wouldn't steal.

He's not that person, I tell myself. Not anymore.

So why did he slip out in the night?

That's a question I may never know the answer to. Back to the kitchen. As I'm filling the teakettle to heat water for the French press, there's a knock at the door.

My breath catches. I don't want to get my hopes up. It's probably not him. Rather, it might be a neighbor asking to borrow a cup of sugar, a motorist with no GPS wanting directions to the Fremont Troll statue. My mugger from the night before…

I can't help it, though. My heart quickens with glad anticipation as I hurry to the front door. I check through the peephole and then fling the door open. My smile widens. It's him! He's holding a brown paper sack and grinning back.

"Good morning," he says.

"Where did you go?" I ask. I poke his chest a little, and he steps back. "I was worried."

"Good morning," he repeats, gazing at me a little more intently.

I frown, and then a light goes on. I smile again and open the door a little wider. "Good morning," I answer and step back a little. "Do you want to come in?"

"I do," he says. He steps in and then shuts the door behind himself.

I turn and start toward the kitchen. "I thought we'd have a little breakfast first."

"First? What's second?" Jimmy asks, following.

I feel heat rise to my cheeks as I turn to look over my shoulder at him. "You know," I say, a little sheepish, a little embarrassed.

This is fun.

And real.

And part of me wants to laugh and the other to cry, but happy tears.

"Okay. I'm not so stupid."

We both end up in the kitchen, where he sets his little brown paper bag on the counter. It's a joyful yet awkward moment. To get things moving, I point to the bag. "Whatcha got there?"

"Something that was missing that morning our paths crossed in the diner just a few days ago."

I reach out a hand to grab for the bag, and he moves it out of my reach.

"You remember that morning in the diner? When you kidded around with me?" Jimmy asks. "Playing out some silly routine from kids' public television, I think it was. Yeah, I know public TV for kids. I grew up with it. Sometimes I think my real parent, and my best friend, back in those days was the television set."

I nod. I remember playing out that whole little stupid routine. "I'll have coffee and a cinnamon roll," I say softly.

"But, but..." He looks to be searching for the right words. When they come to him, I know because his breath catches. He holds up a finger. "You wanted me to give you something I didn't have to give."

I cock my head. I nod. I think I know where this is going. "Kind of like that very first night, so long ago."

Jimmy looks down at the floor. "Yeah."

"I wanted you to give me something you didn't have to give," I say. "But I think if you did have it to give, you would've, Jimmy." I feel the sadness, a poignant nudge to my heart, rise up. I pick up the brown paper bag off the counter.

"Oh yes," he sighs. "In my heart, I knew I wanted to."

"The idea of giving me love was so scary, you didn't know what to do with it. And I don't know if I was ready—" I stop myself. "No. I wasn't ready either." I open the bag. "Not for anything sweet."

I peer inside the bag, and there's a quartet of Schwartz cinnamon rolls at the bottom. I smile. I close my eyes, feel the emotion rise. My heart swells.

Jimmy says, "You'll have coffee and a—?"

"Cinnamon roll."

I put the bag down. And suddenly we are in each other's arms, squeezing. Clinging to the other as if we're each other's very salvation.

And we are. And we are.

I lean in to kiss him, and he presses a hand to my chest. "Wait." He reaches into the bag, takes out the plastic container of cinnamon rolls. He opens them and, with his hands, tears one off from the rest. "Take a bite?"

I do, and he follows me, taking his own bite.

When we kiss, we taste of cream cheese frosting. And something even sweeter.

Chapter Twenty-One

MIRIAM

I watch the boys from my perch on the kitchen counter. I'm smiling, even though there's a tear in my eye. I feel as though I've raised Jimmy even more than I raised my own children. And he's grown up now, a man. A man I can be proud of. He's faced his demons and come out on the other side whole.

I wish I could give him a hug and a chip. Pat him on the back for being the man I always knew he could be.

They make silly for a while, smearing the cream cheese frosting from the cinnamon rolls on each other's faces and lips, licking it off and laughing. There are those mumbled declarations of love that lovers make when they feel secure, when they know for certain something sweet and good and true is coming.

When they feel safe.

I slide down from the counter as their clothes begin to come off, landing on the tile floor in a heap. What remains of the frosting moves to body parts farther south from lips and necks.

I move through the little apartment, grabbing a final glimpse of the world outside the windows as I do. The sunlight, the mountains, the water.

At the front door, I pause. They have too. Jimmy is saying, "Before we go any further, I should tell you—my name is Jimmy."

"And I'm Marc."

I watch as they come together again, almost like one being.

It's beautiful.

New beginnings.

I turn, closing out the sounds of their lovemaking as I know they're sinking to the floor.

I had my hand on the doorknob, but I change course and move toward the window instead. I near the glass and pass through it, the sunlight warming and then, at last, consuming me.

I vanish into golden light.

About the Author

Real Men. True Love.

Rick R. Reed draws inspiration from the lives of gay men to craft stories that quicken the heartbeat, engage emotions, and keep the pages turning. Although he dabbles in horror, dark suspense, and comedy, his attention always returns to the power of love. He's the award-winning and bestselling author of more than fifty works of published fiction and is forever at work on yet another book. Lambda Literary has called him: "A writer that doesn't disappoint…" You can find him at www.rickrreed.com. Rick lives in Palm Springs, CA with his beloved husband and their fierce Chihuahua/Shiba Inu mix.

Email: rickrreedbooks@gmail.com

Facebook: www.facebook.com/rickrreedbooks

Twitter: @rickrreed

Website: www.rickrreed.com

Other books by this author

Unraveling

Sky Full of Mysteries

Coming Soon from Rick R Reed

IM

When Tony logged on to the Men4HookUpNow website, he didn't know this would be the last time he would type in his screen name and password, the last time he would scroll through thumbnail-sized pictures of men in various states of undress, or the last time he would read an instant message.

Tony didn't know logging on to Men4HookUpNow.com would be one of the last things he would do.

Ever.

The simple blue-and-white instant message box was a blank canvas, containing only a list of provocative screen names: musclestud, pnpjock, pozpup4u… And any one of these screen names could spring to life by sending Tony an instant message or, as everyone called them, an IM. Anyone could arrive within its simple frame: a college football player, a construction worker, a truck driver, or just a man in tight jeans and engineer boots.

There was a pinging sound, and a message appeared on the screen. Tony leaned forward to see who had come to call.

And *whoosh*, a real man came through cyberspace, delivered like a gift. The box held only one word, "Hi," yet Tony felt its author could see through his monitor, see him there in his living room wearing only a pair of boxer shorts, see the porno playing on his TV screen.

"Come on, man," Tony whispered, fingers poised above the keyboard. "Hi? Can't you do better than that?" He wanted someone with a bit more personality this languid August night, so he hit the Delete key and banished the guy into limbo, where someone else might take his "Hi" with a little more encouragement. Tony began a scroll through the "Available Now" guys, reading the inane descriptions ("Let this hot, beefy muscle boy serve you. I'm six two, red hair, green eyes, former All-American football player;" "Aggressive bottom looking for well-endowed top men. I'm into just about everything except for scat, and I know how to take orders;" "Looking to party with a hot stud;" "Straight-appearing and acting;" "Negative... UB2") and stopping if one of the thumbnails caught his eye, especially if the guy had the courage to show his face.

Tony idly stroked himself as the images paraded past. He asked himself why he was bothering with going online. For Christ's sake, here it was, Saturday night. Couldn't he throw on some jeans and head down to Halsted Street? At least in a bar, he would know for sure what the guy looked like if they decided to hook up, rather than seeing a cock shot and hoping the guy had a nice face or trusting a face pic a decade old. This way, all he had to work with was exaggeration, living in a world where "stocky" and "football-player build" meant fat, where thirty-eight-year-olds tried to pass as twenty-nine, where any bald guy could lay claim to looking like Bruce Willis, where average meant so hideous you might as well hide under a rock.

The instant message box popped up.

"Hey, what's up?"

Well, at least better than "Hi."

Tony keyed in: "Just real horny. Looking to hook up." If the horny part weren't so true, Tony wouldn't have been able to keep himself from laughing. Trying to put a macho façade on his typed words, trying to make himself sound like he had an eighth-grade education made him feel idiotic. A queer Stanley Kowalski.

"Know what you mean, dude."

So the guy was playing the macho game with him.

"So, man, what do you look like?"

"Twenty-four. Black. Blue. Nice lean muscular build, work out about three or four times a week. Nicely defined pecs. Good tan. Hairy chest. Eight inches cut, real thick. You?"

Tony felt himself transported. It was like the guy got into his head, reading the ingredients for his perfect fantasy man. His dick started to rise with anticipation, and he found his hand moving up and down the length of it, almost of its own accord. He clicked on the guy's screen name on the instant messenger list, jock4play, and was disappointed to see no pictures in his profile. Still, if the description was accurate... Tony typed in: "Yeah, I'm twenty-eight. I've got dark blond hair, green eyes, moustache, goatee. Smooth swimmer's build. Work out a lot too. Um. Got about seven, cut, shaved balls. Check out my pics."

"You a top or bottom?" There wasn't even a pause, so Tony wondered if the guy had bothered to look.

"Pretty open. I like it all. Very versatile. How about you? What are you into?"

"I'm a top, dude. Lookin' for a good bottom boy."

"I can do that."

"Yeah?"

"Sure. Whereabouts are you, man?"

"North Side."

"Yeah, me too. I'm in Rogers Park, Touhy and Ashland."

"I'm not too far from you."

Tony swallowed his common sense as the image of his fantasy man took over. "You wanna come over?"

"You like to party?"

"Yeah." Tony loved little more than getting high and getting down. "Tina's here." Tony eyed the little glass pipe, its bottom crusted with black residue and white powder. His nerves—right along with his libido—were in overdrive.

"Poppers?"

"Got 'em."

"Hmmm. I could be interested."

Tony looked briefly at the TV, where a hairy-chested drill sergeant had a lithe blond "private" bent over his desk. He wanted to get things moving, so he typed: "You wanna call me?"

"Sure. Number?"

"My cell is 555-7654. Call me right back. Okay?" Was that too pushy? Many times they never bothered to call. Many times they said they would show up and never did. But once in a while, it all came together.

His cell chirped. He flipped it open. "Hey."

"What's goin' on, dude?"

"God, I just need some dick. You interested in hookin' up, man?"

"The sooner the better."

"Got somethin' to write with?" And Tony got busy, giving precise directions to his apartment.

Precise directions to a stranger.

After he hung up, Tony felt flushed, a deep burning radiating from chest to face. His heart pounded as if he had just done a big hit of poppers. God, the guy sounded incredible! He suddenly knew why he was doing this as opposed to going out to a bar. When the site worked, it worked. There was no bullshit, no game playing. No eye contact for an hour, no fumbling for something to say and then sounding like a dork. When it worked with the site, it was simply two lusting men getting together and pleasuring each other. They didn't need to say a word. *Then why not a bathhouse?* Tony asked himself, wandering around the apartment, folding up newspapers and throwing magazines in the wicker basket he stored them in. He remembered Man Universe and the last time he was there. It was okay, he guessed; there wasn't the usual amount of bullshit. He thought with a grin of the open doors and the guys lying within, naked on their stomachs, the white moons of their asses a focal point, the bottles of lube and poppers on the little tables beside the beds. But the bathhouse lacked one thing the Men4HookUpNow offered: the element of surprise. Having someone show up after making an online connection, there was always that breathless moment when you opened the door to see what you were getting. Even if you had seen photos, it was always a crapshoot. A grab bag. And that's what made it so exciting. The gamble made the rewards all the sweeter. And, hey, if you lost one time, you just said "Sorry," closed the door, and got back online.

There was no shortage of hot guys online.

Or at least adequate ones.

Tony glanced at himself as he passed the mirror in his

dining room, grateful he had worked out earlier in the day, grateful for the fact that he never had to exaggerate. His blond hair was buzzed, and his muscles had good definition. His lips were slightly pouty, giving his face an aura of innocence defiled... Details in his face combined to form a very pleasing contradiction: sleazy and at the same time babyish, childlike.

Tony never lacked for admirers.

And sometimes he wished he did. He thought of *him*, the asshole who was always around, the one who, after three dates, couldn't handle his request to be just friends.

But think of that another time! A party was coming up. And Tony wanted to make sure this party was of the all-night variety.

He headed for the kitchen to take the poppers out of the freezer. He held the little brown glass bottle up to the light and shook it. It was about at the halfway point, certainly enough to see him through the evening.

In the bedroom, he placed a couple of towels on the nightstand, along with a bottle of Wet. At the portable CD player, he put in Delirium—great fuck music—and he made sure the votive candles were adequate enough to burn for the hours he planned on taking with this guy, if he was as good as he sounded.

Tony turned to the mirror once more, running his hand through the blond spikes, making them stand on end. He flexed his biceps and was pleased at the image the mirror threw back.

He reached in his dresser drawer, pulled out his metal cock ring, and slid it over his dick and balls. He strapped a metal band with studs around his right arm "Perfect," he whispered to his grinning reflection.

Blood pounded in his ears. A line of sweat formed at

his hairline and under his arms.

He couldn't wait.

The buzzer sounded.

Tony walked slowly to the intercom box in the front hallway, not wanting to appear too eager. Desperation was never pretty.

It sounded once more before he placed his hand on the Talk button. "Yeah?"

"It's your buddy from online."

Tony pressed the button marked Door and then the one marked Listen so he could hear the guy coming in. He hoped he wouldn't be disappointed.

It was hard to tell, but the guy's voice didn't sound quite as deep as he thought it had when the guy called his cell. Perhaps the intercom was just distorting his voice a bit.

But there was something else. No, it couldn't be...but the voice had a familiar cast to it. Tony wondered when the day would come when he ran into someone he knew from Men4HookUpNow.

Perhaps the day was today.

But the familiarity of the voice didn't have pleasant associations.

Imagination. *Tony, bud, you're imagining things.*

Anyway, there was no time to think about that now, not with the guy tapping on his door.

Tony peered through the peephole.

And saw nothing.

He didn't like that. But the guy was probably standing to the left or right of the hole, that's all. Good sense deserted Tony, usurped by lust.

He opened the door, and the color drained from his face. "What the hell are *you* doing here?"

Also Available from NineStar Press

Connect with NineStar Press

www.ninestarpress.com

www.facebook.com/ninestarpress

www.facebook.com/groups/NineStarNiche

www.twitter.com/ninestarpress

www.tumblr.com/blog/ninestarpress